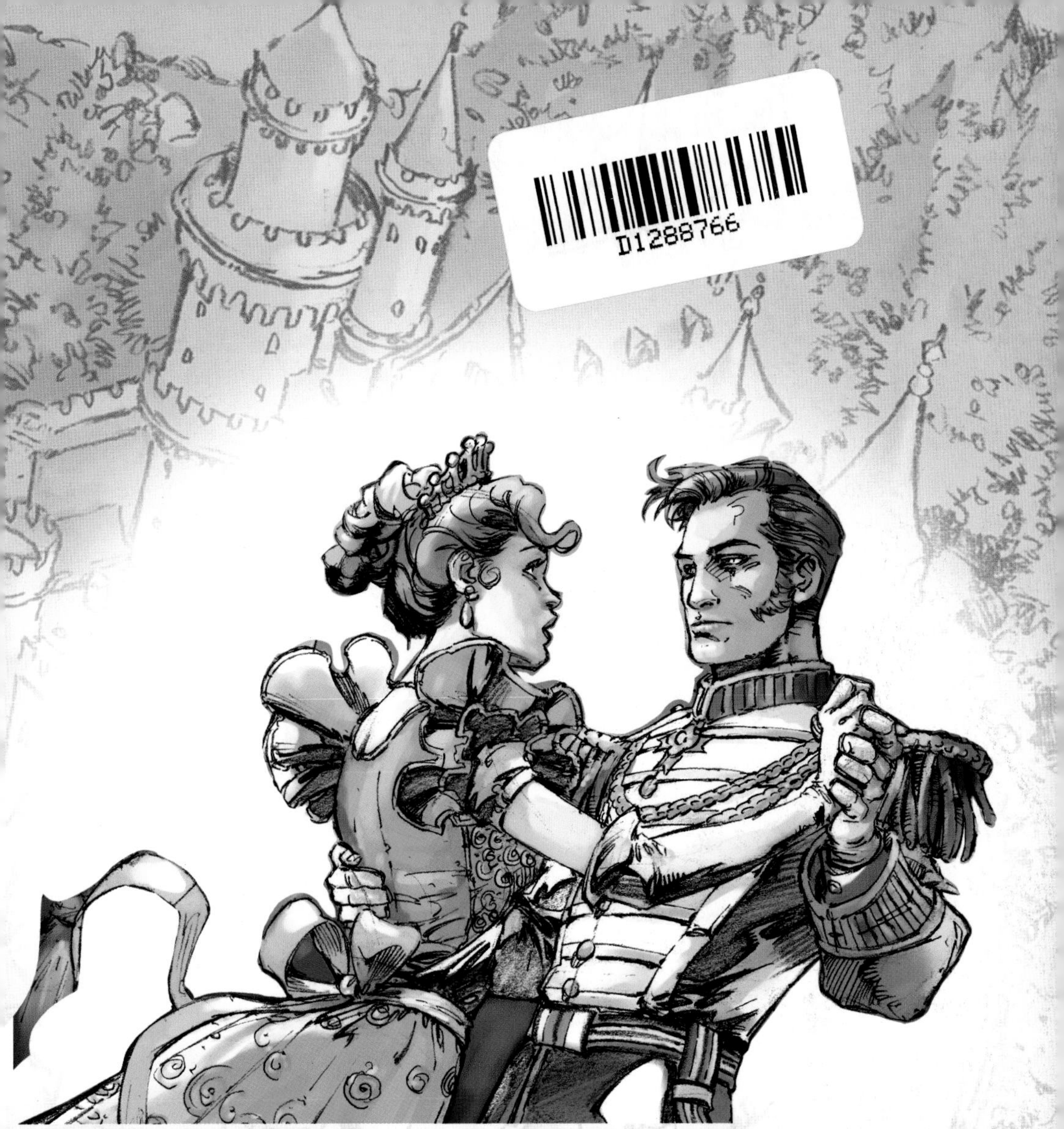

THE PRISONER OF ZENDA

CAMPFIRE™

KALYANI NAVYUG MEDIA PVT LTD
NEW DELHI

Sitting around the Campfire, telling the story, were:

Wordsmith	:	Lloyd S. Wagner
Illustrator	:	Lalit Kumar Sharma
Illustrations Editor	:	Jayshree Das
Colorists	:	Vijay Sharma/Prince Varghese
Letterers	:	Bhavnath Chaudhary
		Vishal Sharma
Editors	:	Eman Choudhary
		Andrew Dodd
Editor (Information Content)	:	Pushpanjali Borooah
Production Controller	:	Vishal Sharma

Cover Artists:

Illustrator	:	Lalit Sharma
Colorist	:	Jaya Krishnan K. P.
Designer	:	Jaya Krishnan K. P.

Published by Kalyani Navyug Media Pvt Ltd
101 C, Shiv House, Hari Nagar Ashram
New Delhi 110014
India
www.campfire.co.in

ISBN: 978-93-80028-28-6

Copyright © 2010 Kalyani Navyug Media Pvt Ltd

All rights reserved. Published by Campfire, an imprint of Kalyani Navyug Media Pvt Ltd.

No part of this publication may be reproduced, stored in a retrieval system, or transmitted in any form or by any means, electronic, mechanical, photocopying, recording, or otherwise, without written permission from the publisher.

Printed in India at Tara Art Printers Pvt Ltd.

ABOUT THE AUTHOR

Anthony Hope was the pen name of Sir Anthony Hope Hawkins. Born in London on February 9,1863, Hope studied at the prestigious Marlborough School before attending Balliol College, Oxford University. He received a first-class degree and, in 1887, went to work as a lawyer. An ambitious man, Hope began writing stories in his free time and published his first novel, *A Man of Mark*, in 1890. Most of his novels were adventure stories, typified by *The Prisoner of Zenda*, his best-known work.

Hope started work on *The Prisoner of Zenda* in November 1893, and finished writing it within a month. The book was published in April 1894 and was an immediate success, receiving praise from such notable literary figures as Robert Louis Stevenson and Andrew Lang.

Based on *The Prisoner of Zenda's* success, Hope gave up his legal career and began writing full time, publishing many popular novels, plays and short stories. *Rupert of Hentzau*, the sequel to *The Prisoner of Zenda*, was published in 1898, and continued where *The Prisoner of Zenda* left off. Among the many books Hope published are *Tristram of Blent* (1901), *Double Harness* (1904), *Sophy of Kravonia* (1906), *The Heart of Princess Osra* (1896) and *Lucinda* (1920).

Hope married Elizabeth Somerville in 1903, and was knighted in 1918 for services to his country during World War I. Sir Anthony Hope Hawkins died at his home in Surrey on July 8, 1933.

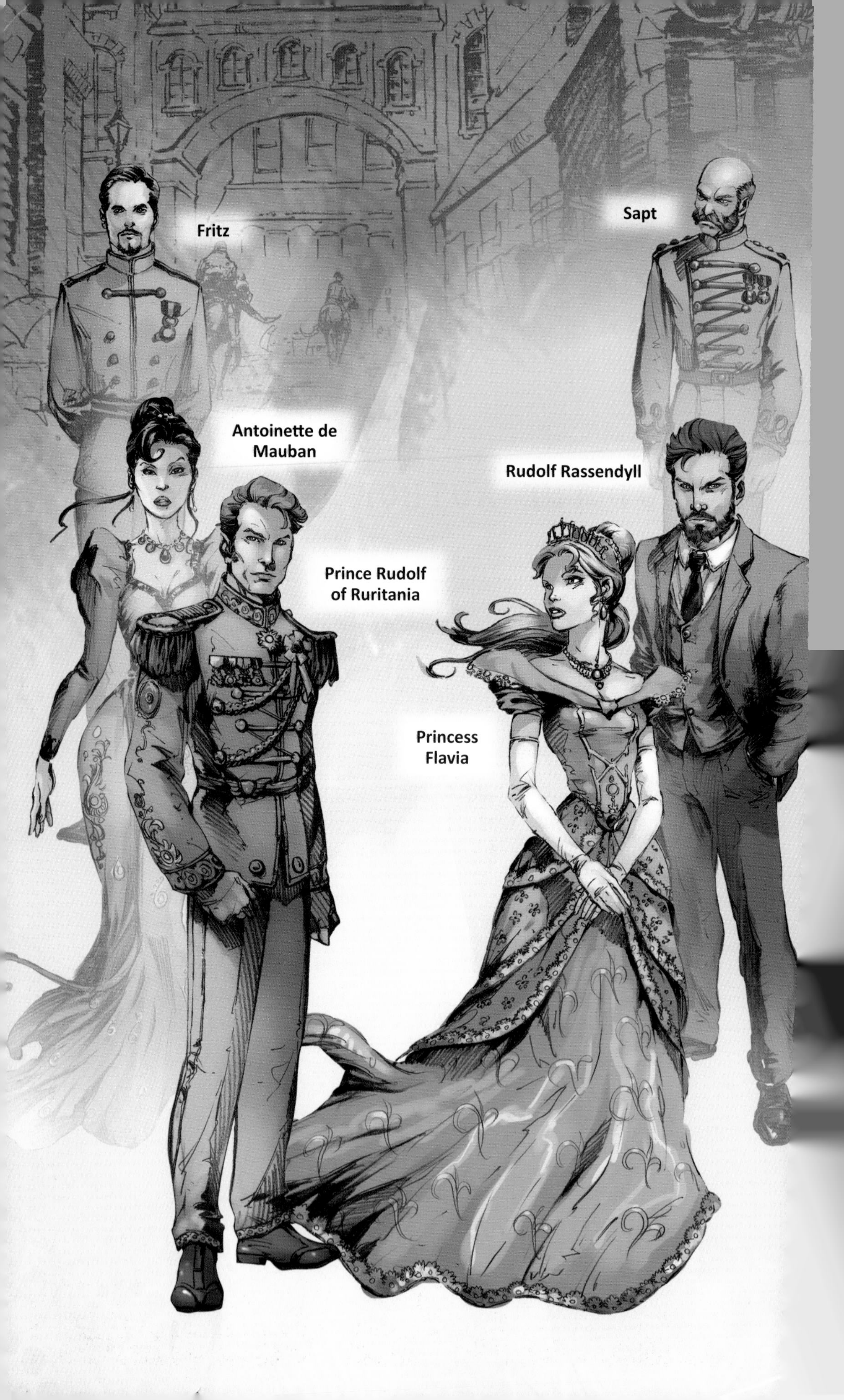
Fritz
Sapt
Antoinette de Mauban
Rudolf Rassendyll
Prince Rudolf of Ruritania
Princess Flavia

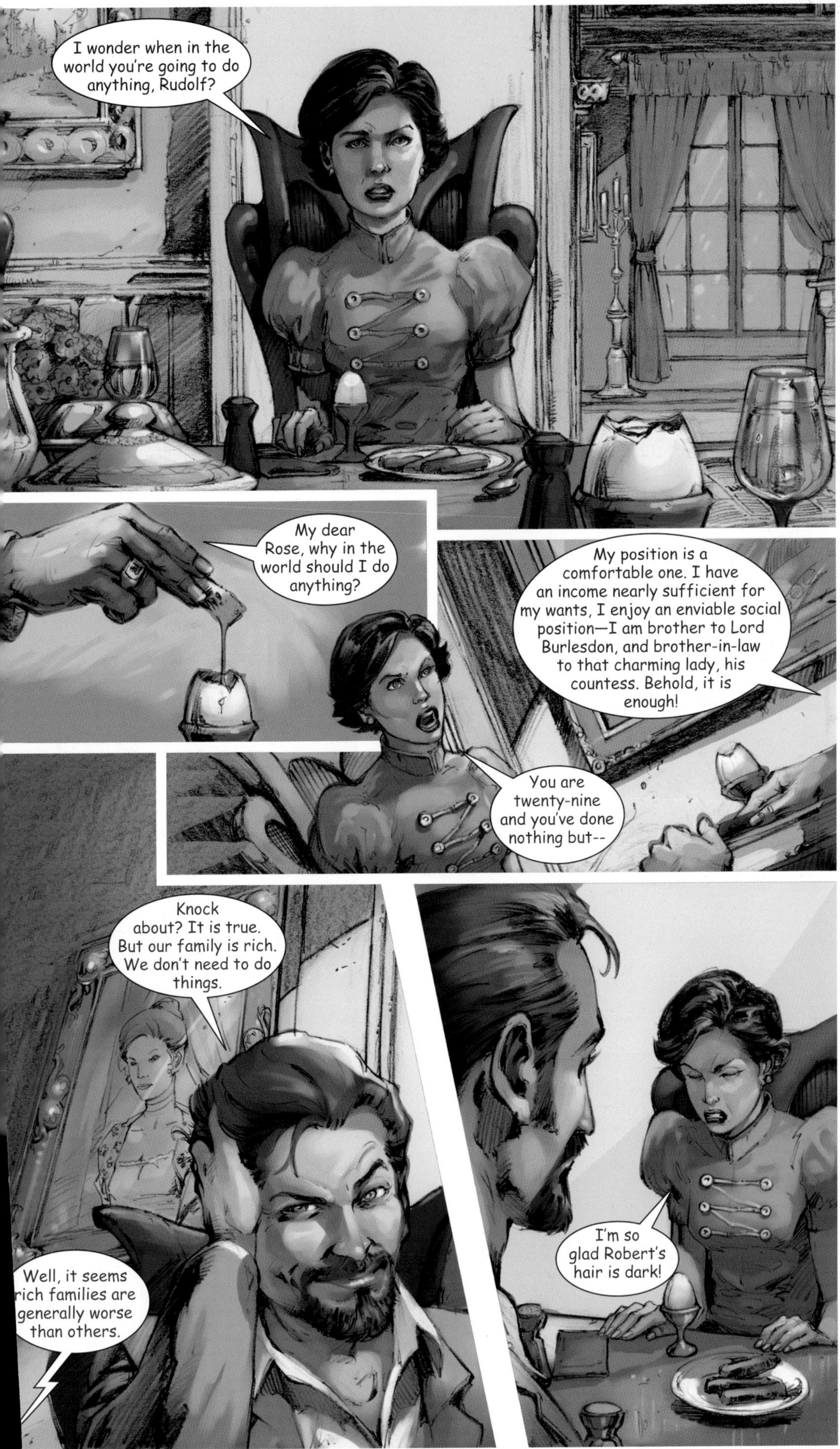
I wonder when in the world you're going to do anything, Rudolf?
My dear Rose, why in the world should I do anything?
My position is a comfortable one. I have an income nearly sufficient for my wants, I enjoy an enviable social position—I am brother to Lord Burlesdon, and brother-in-law to that charming lady, his countess. Behold, it is enough!
You are twenty-nine and you've done nothing but--
Knock about? It is true. But our family is rich. We don't need to do things.
Well, it seems rich families are generally worse than others.
I'm so glad Robert's hair is dark!

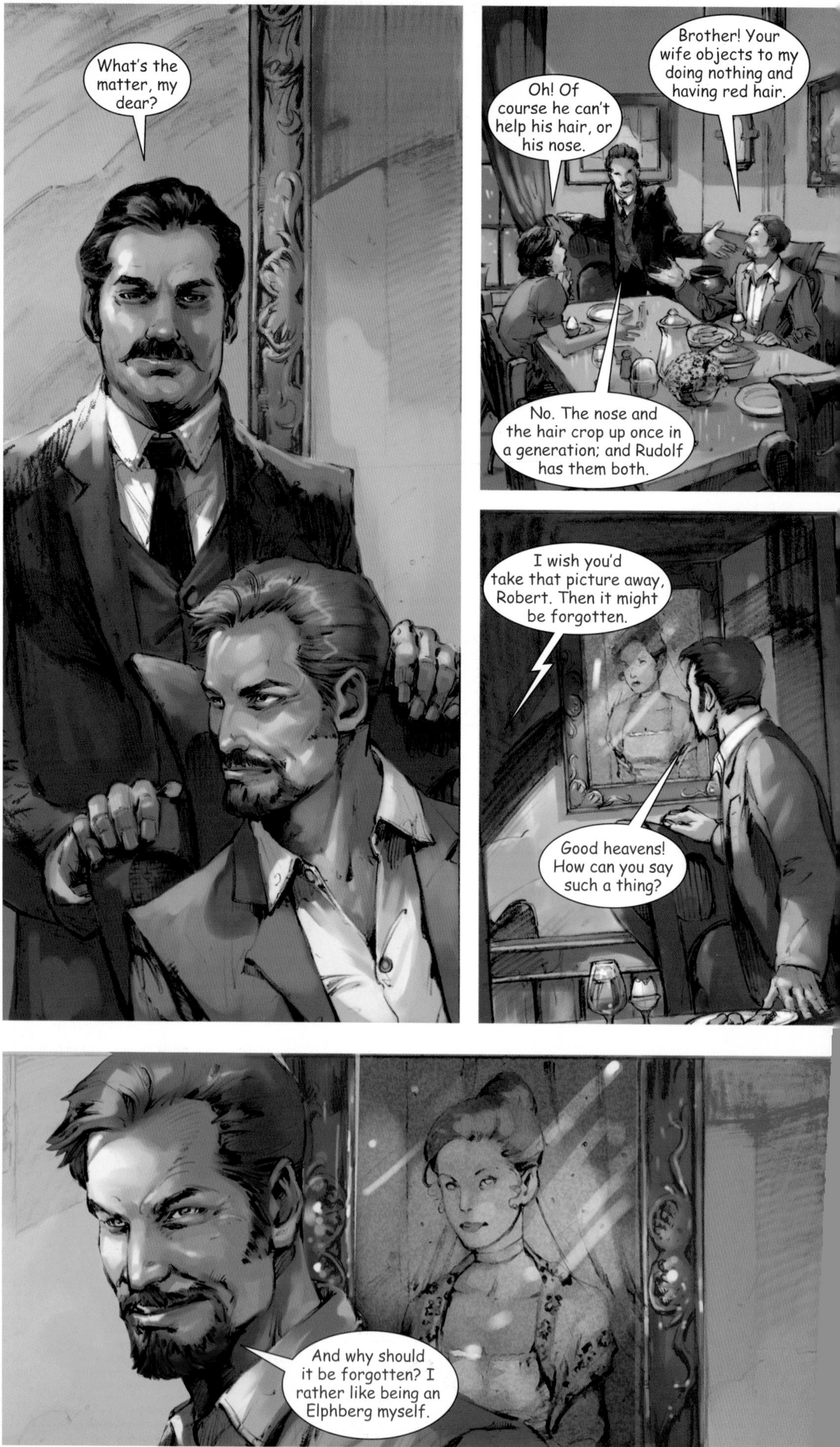

What's the matter, my dear?
Brother! Your wife objects to my doing nothing and having red hair.
Oh! Of course he can't help his hair, or his nose.
No. The nose and the hair crop up once in a generation; and Rudolf has them both.
I wish you'd take that picture away, Robert. Then it might be forgotten.
Good heavens! How can you say such a thing?
And why should it be forgotten? I rather like being an Elphberg myself.

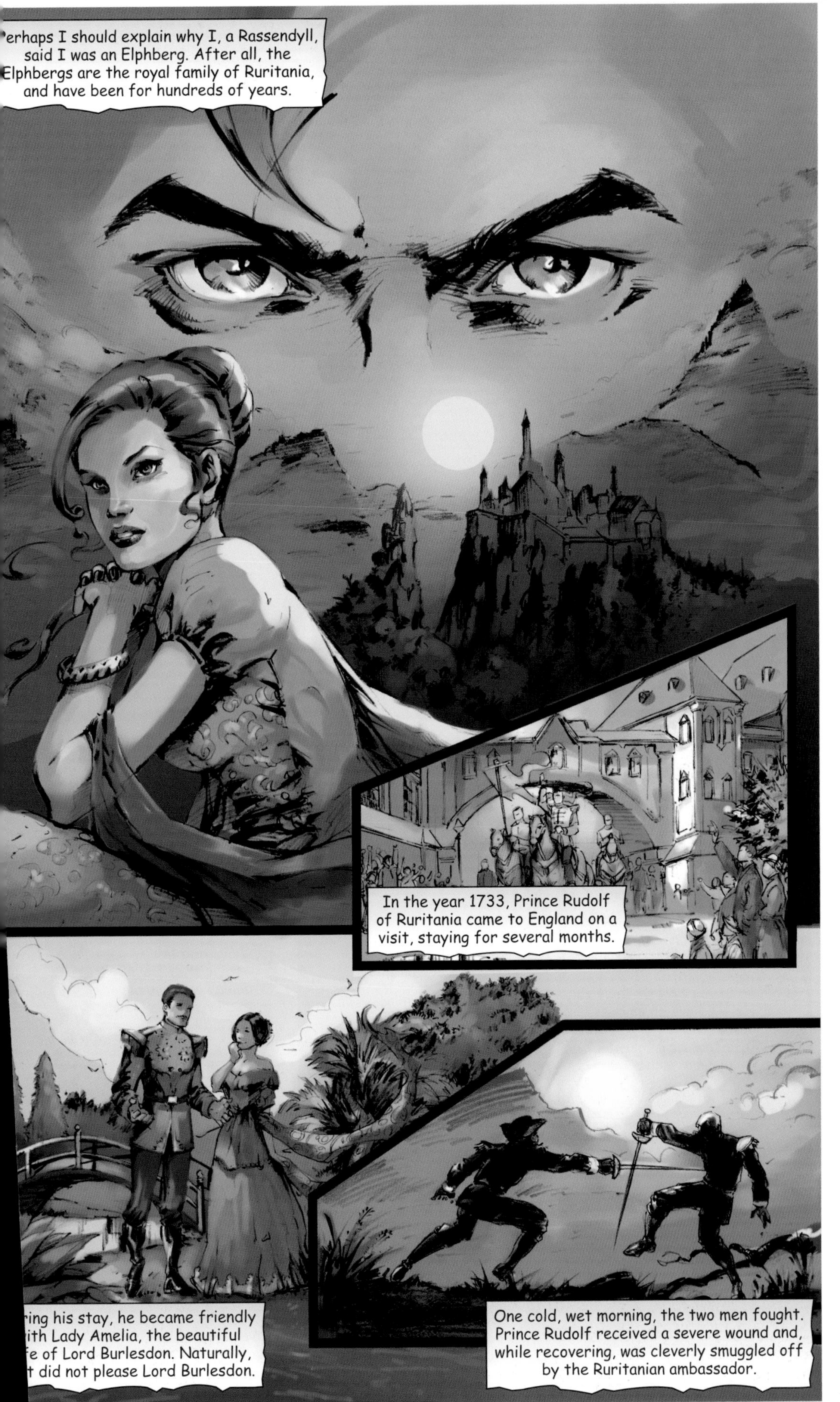
erhaps I should explain why I, a Rassendyll, said I was an Elphberg. After all, the lphbergs are the royal family of Ruritania, and have been for hundreds of years.
In the year 1733, Prince Rudolf of Ruritania came to England on a visit, staying for several months.
ring his stay, he became friendly ith Lady Amelia, the beautiful fe of Lord Burlesdon. Naturally, t did not please Lord Burlesdon.
One cold, wet morning, the two men fought. Prince Rudolf received a severe wound and, while recovering, was cleverly smuggled off by the Ruritanian ambassador.

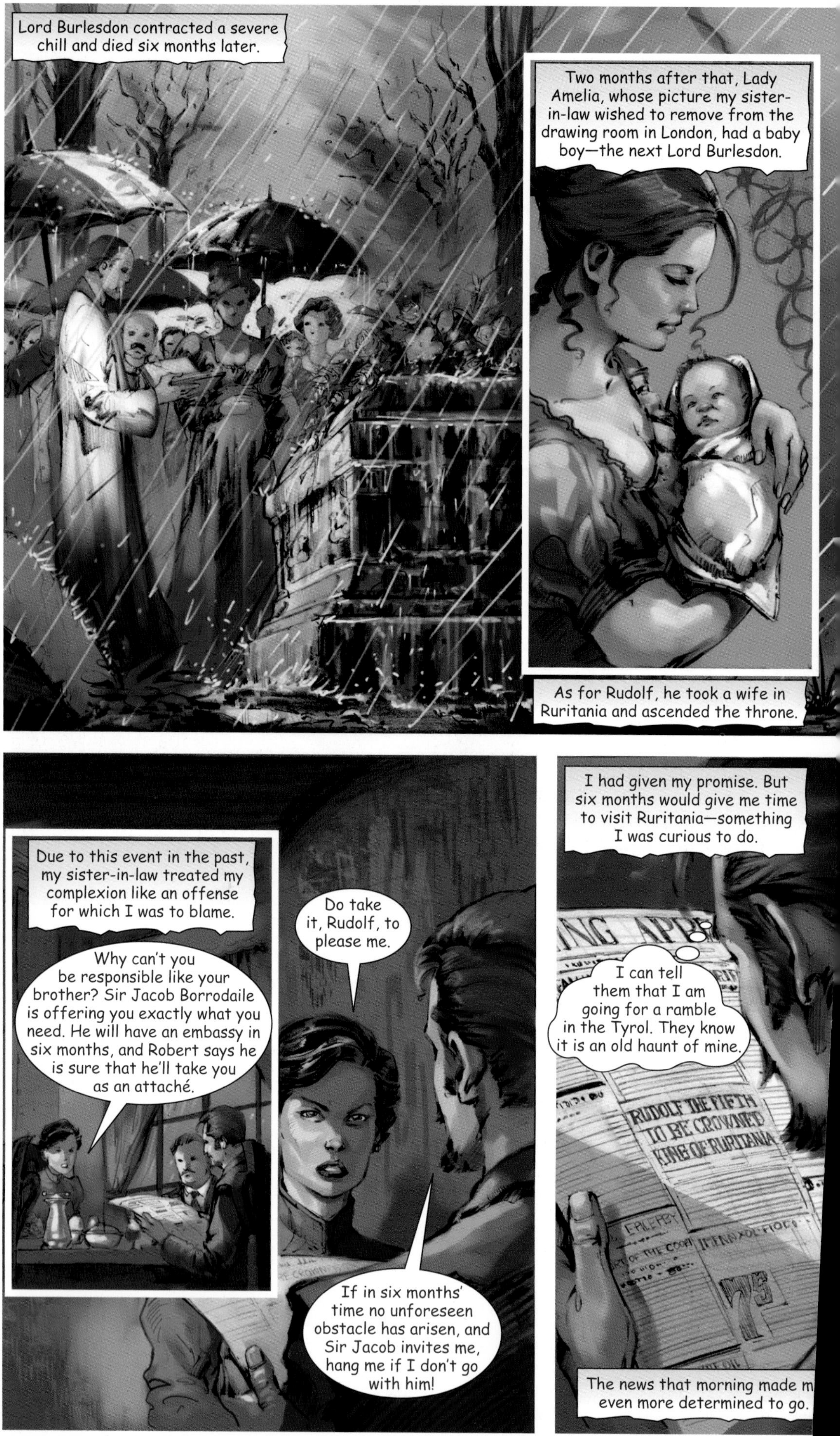
Lord Burlesdon contracted a severe chill and died six months later.
Two months after that, Lady Amelia, whose picture my sister-in-law wished to remove from the drawing room in London, had a baby boy—the next Lord Burlesdon.
As for Rudolf, he took a wife in Ruritania and ascended the throne.
Due to this event in the past, my sister-in-law treated my complexion like an offense for which I was to blame.
Why can't you be responsible like your brother? Sir Jacob Borrodaile is offering you exactly what you need. He will have an embassy in six months, and Robert says he is sure that he'll take you as an attaché.
Do take it, Rudolf, to please me.
If in six months' time no unforeseen obstacle has arisen, and Sir Jacob invites me, hang me if I don't go with him!
I had given my promise. But six months would give me time to visit Ruritania—something I was curious to do.
I can tell them that I am going for a ramble in the Tyrol. They know it is an old haunt of mine.
RUDOLF THE FIFTH TO BE CROWNED KING OF RURITANIA
The news that morning made me even more determined to go.

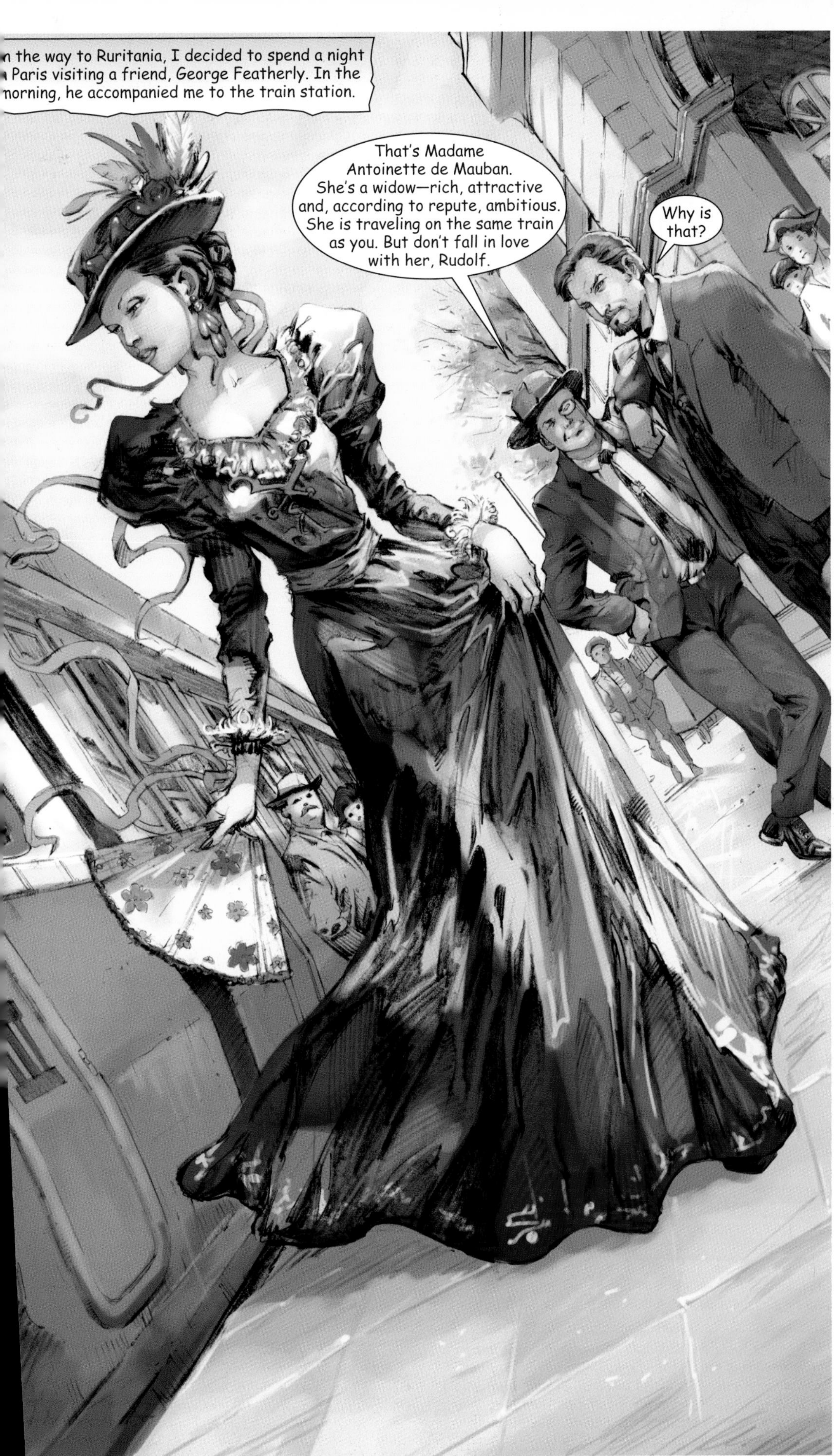
n the way to Ruritania, I decided to spend a night
Paris visiting a friend, George Featherly. In the
morning, he accompanied me to the train station.
That's Madame Antoinette de Mauban. She's a widow—rich, attractive and, according to repute, ambitious. She is traveling on the same train as you. But don't fall in love with her, Rudolf.
Why is that?

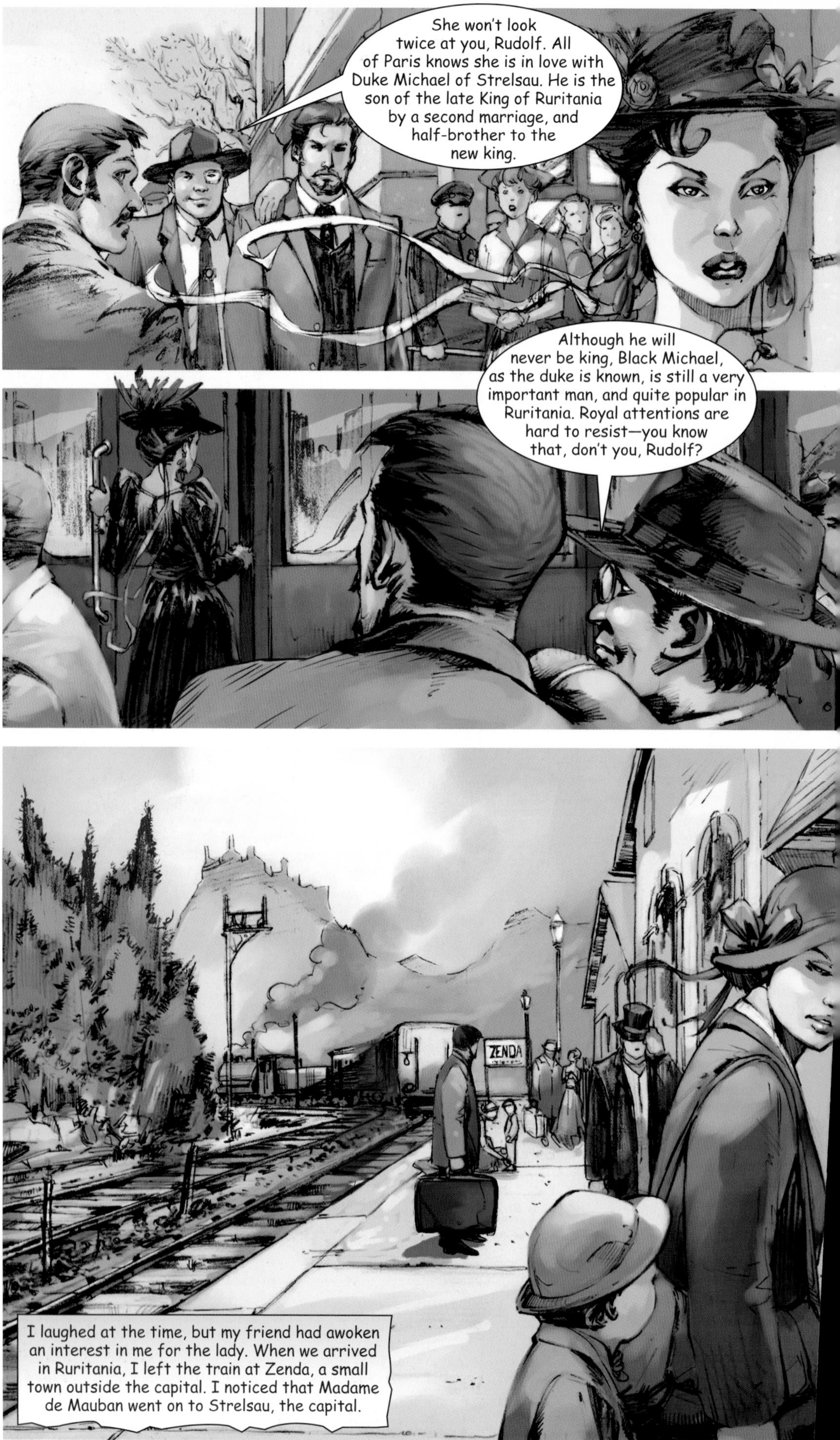
She won't look twice at you, Rudolf. All of Paris knows she is in love with Duke Michael of Strelsau. He is the son of the late King of Ruritania by a second marriage, and half-brother to the new king.
Although he will never be king, Black Michael, as the duke is known, is still a very important man, and quite popular in Ruritania. Royal attentions are hard to resist—you know that, don't you, Rudolf?
ZENDA
I laughed at the time, but my friend had awoken an interest in me for the lady. When we arrived in Ruritania, I left the train at Zenda, a small town outside the capital. I noticed that Madame de Mauban went on to Strelsau, the capital.

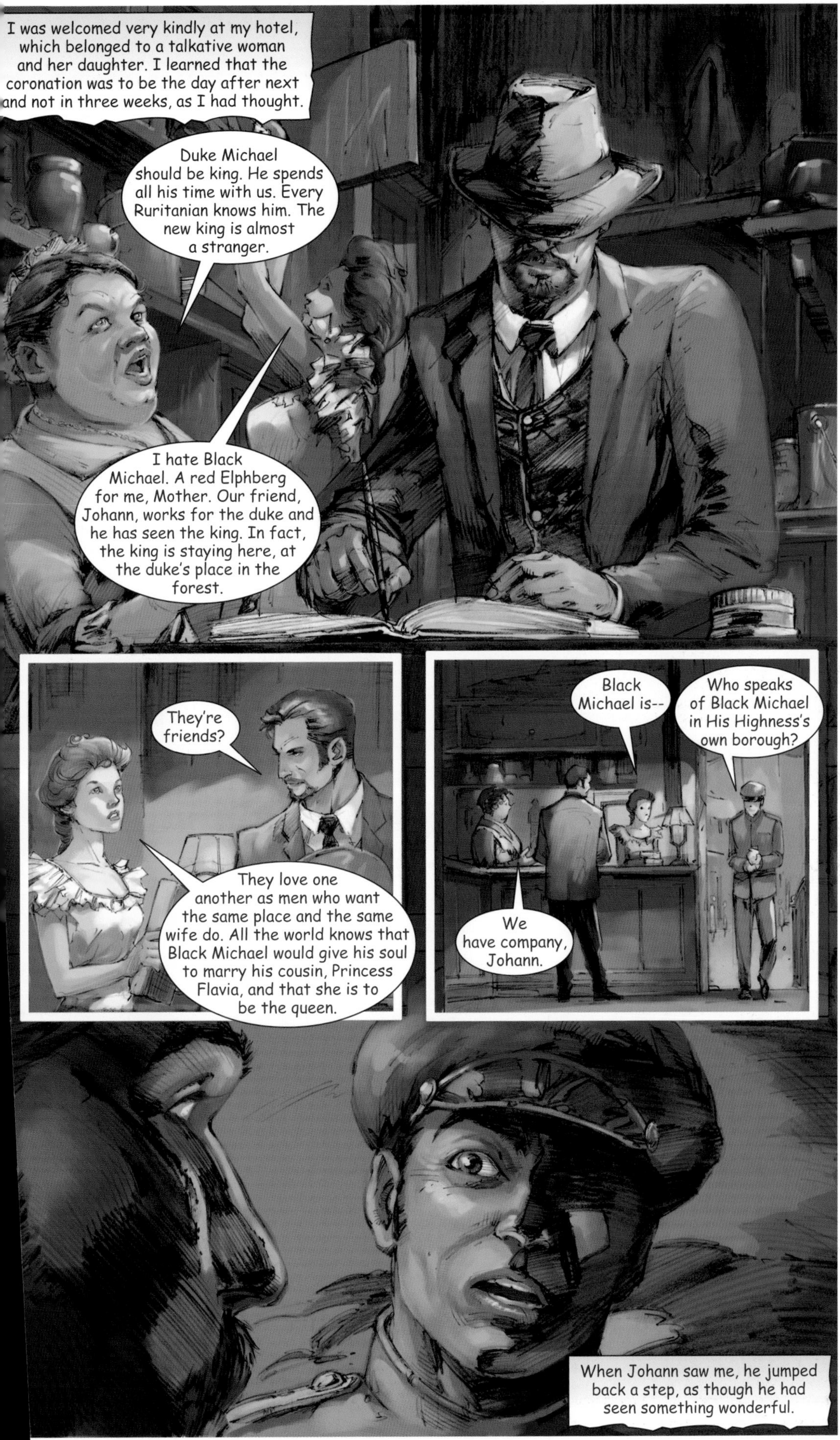
I was welcomed very kindly at my hotel, which belonged to a talkative woman and her daughter. I learned that the coronation was to be the day after next and not in three weeks, as I had thought.
Duke Michael should be king. He spends all his time with us. Every Ruritanian knows him. The new king is almost a stranger.
I hate Black Michael. A red Elphberg for me, Mother. Our friend, Johann, works for the duke and he has seen the king. In fact, the king is staying here, at the duke's place in the forest.
They're friends?
They love one another as men who want the same place and the same wife do. All the world knows that Black Michael would give his soul to marry his cousin, Princess Flavia, and that she is to be the queen.
Black Michael is--
Who speaks of Black Michael in His Highness's own borough?
We have company, Johann.
When Johann saw me, he jumped back a step, as though he had seen something wonderful.

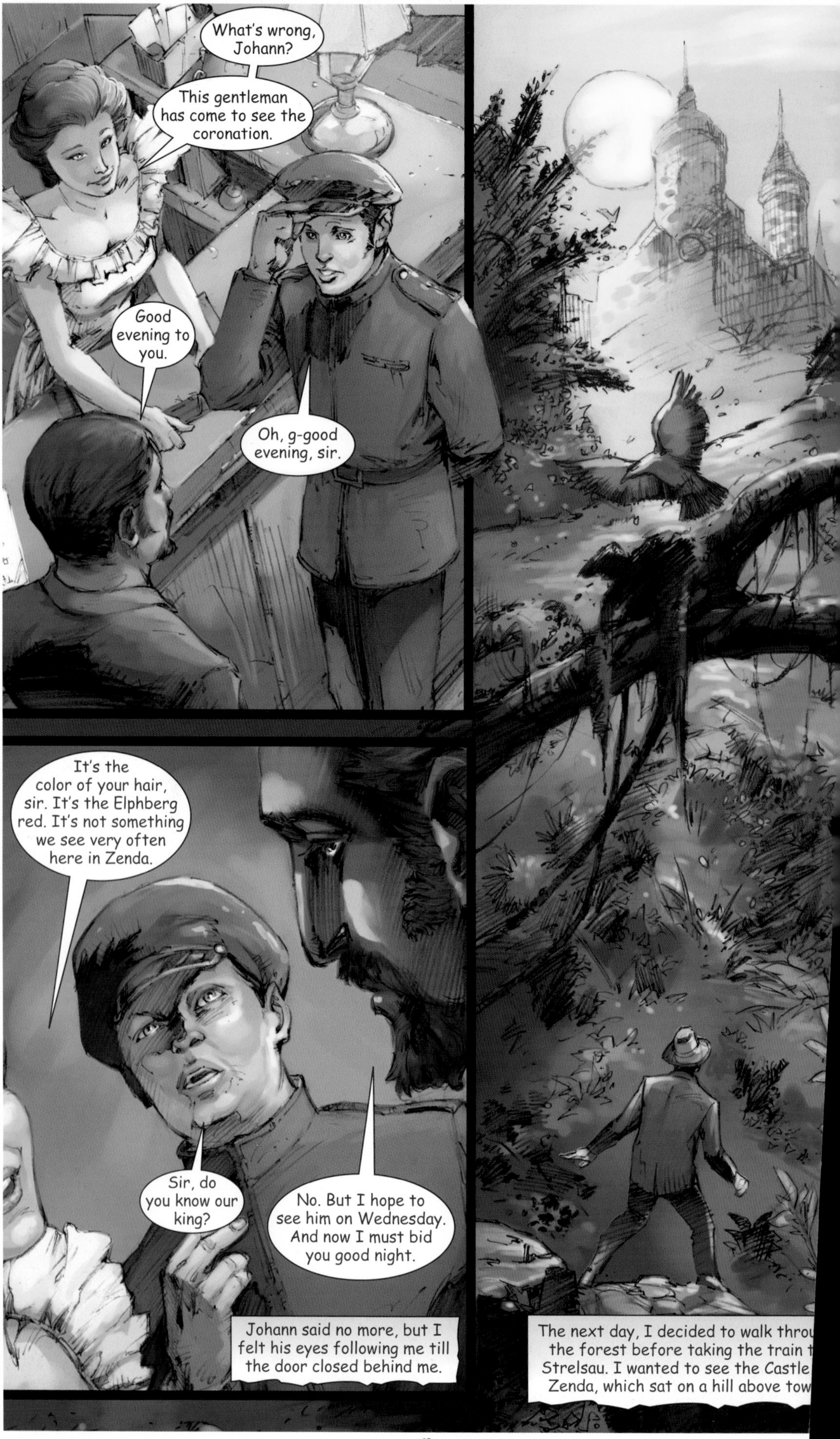
What's wrong, Johann?
This gentleman has come to see the coronation.
Good evening to you.
Oh, g-good evening, sir.
It's the color of your hair, sir. It's the Elphberg red. It's not something we see very often here in Zenda.
Sir, do you know our king?
No. But I hope to see him on Wednesday. And now I must bid you good night.
Johann said no more, but I felt his eyes following me till the door closed behind me.
The next day, I decided to walk throu
the forest before taking the train t
Strelsau. I wanted to see the Castle
Zenda, which sat on a hill above tow

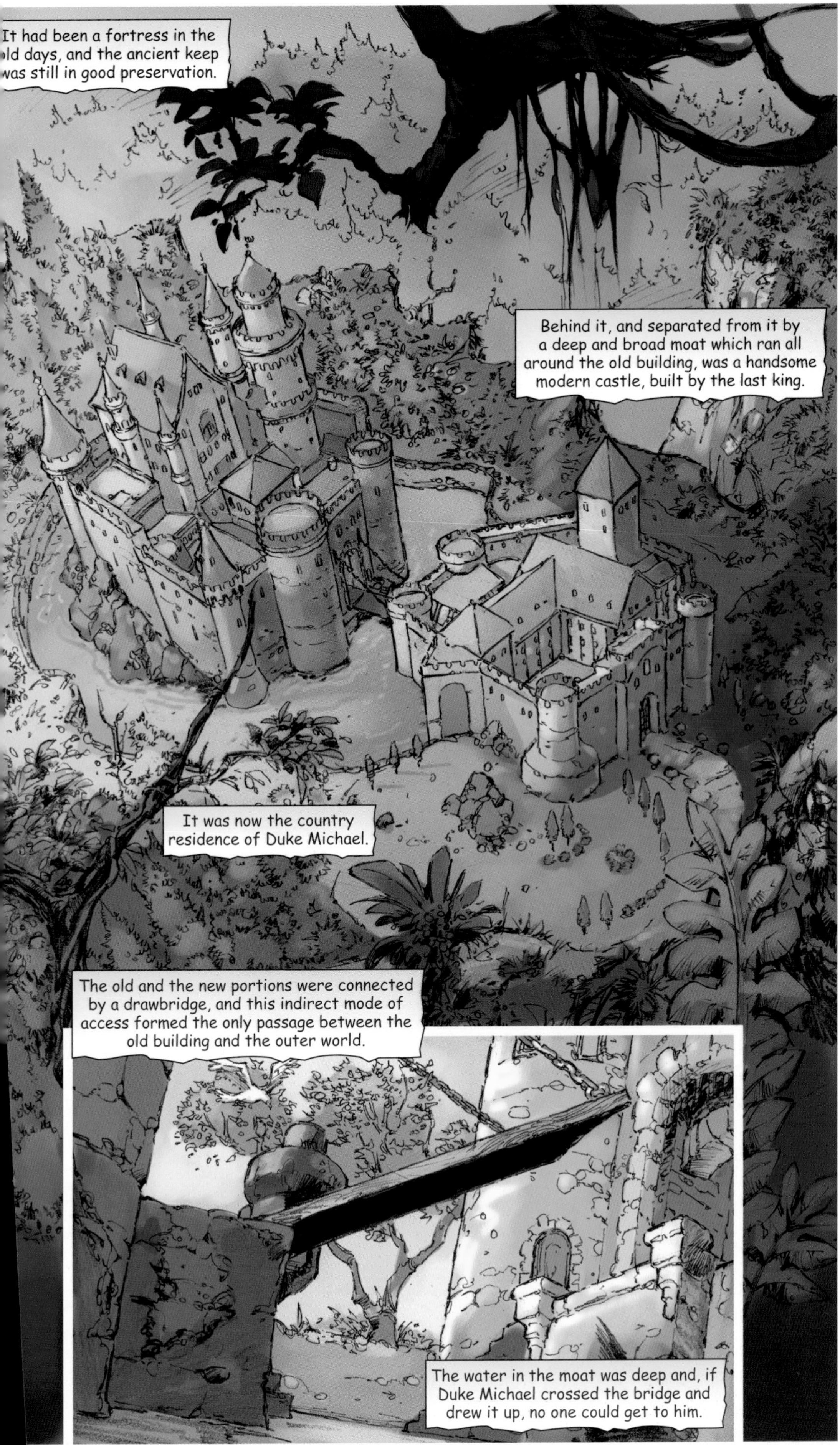
It had been a fortress in the old days, and the ancient keep was still in good preservation.
Behind it, and separated from it by a deep and broad moat which ran all around the old building, was a handsome modern castle, built by the last king.
It was now the country residence of Duke Michael.
The old and the new portions were connected by a drawbridge, and this indirect mode of access formed the only passage between the old building and the outer world.
The water in the moat was deep and, if Duke Michael crossed the bridge and drew it up, no one could get to him.

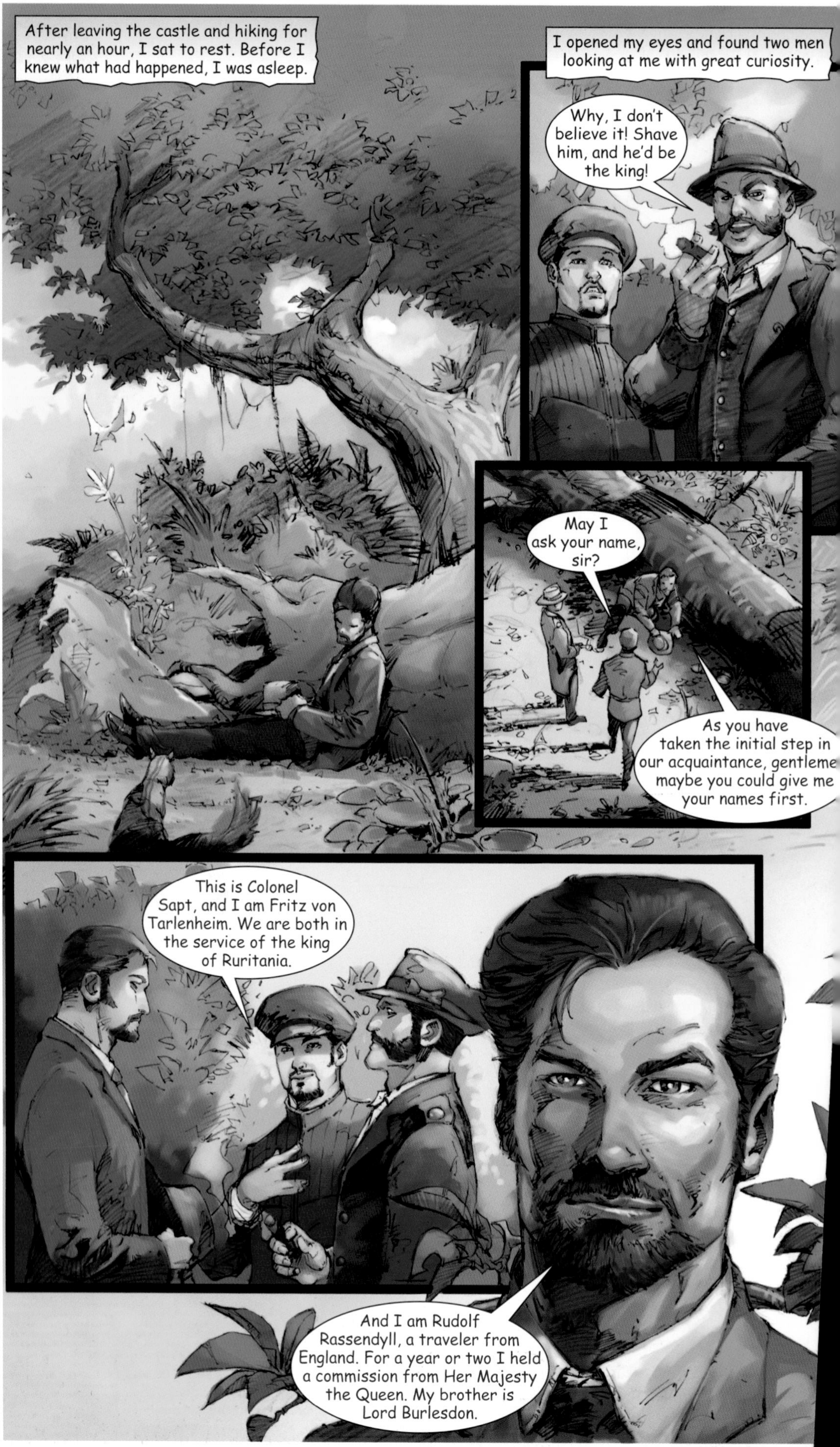
After leaving the castle and hiking for nearly an hour, I sat to rest. Before I knew what had happened, I was asleep.
I opened my eyes and found two men looking at me with great curiosity.
Why, I don't believe it! Shave him, and he'd be the king!
May I ask your name, sir?
As you have taken the initial step in our acquaintance, gentleme maybe you could give me your names first.
This is Colonel Sapt, and I am Fritz von Tarlenheim. We are both in the service of the king of Ruritania.
And I am Rudolf Rassendyll, a traveler from England. For a year or two I held a commission from Her Majesty the Queen. My brother is Lord Burlesdon.

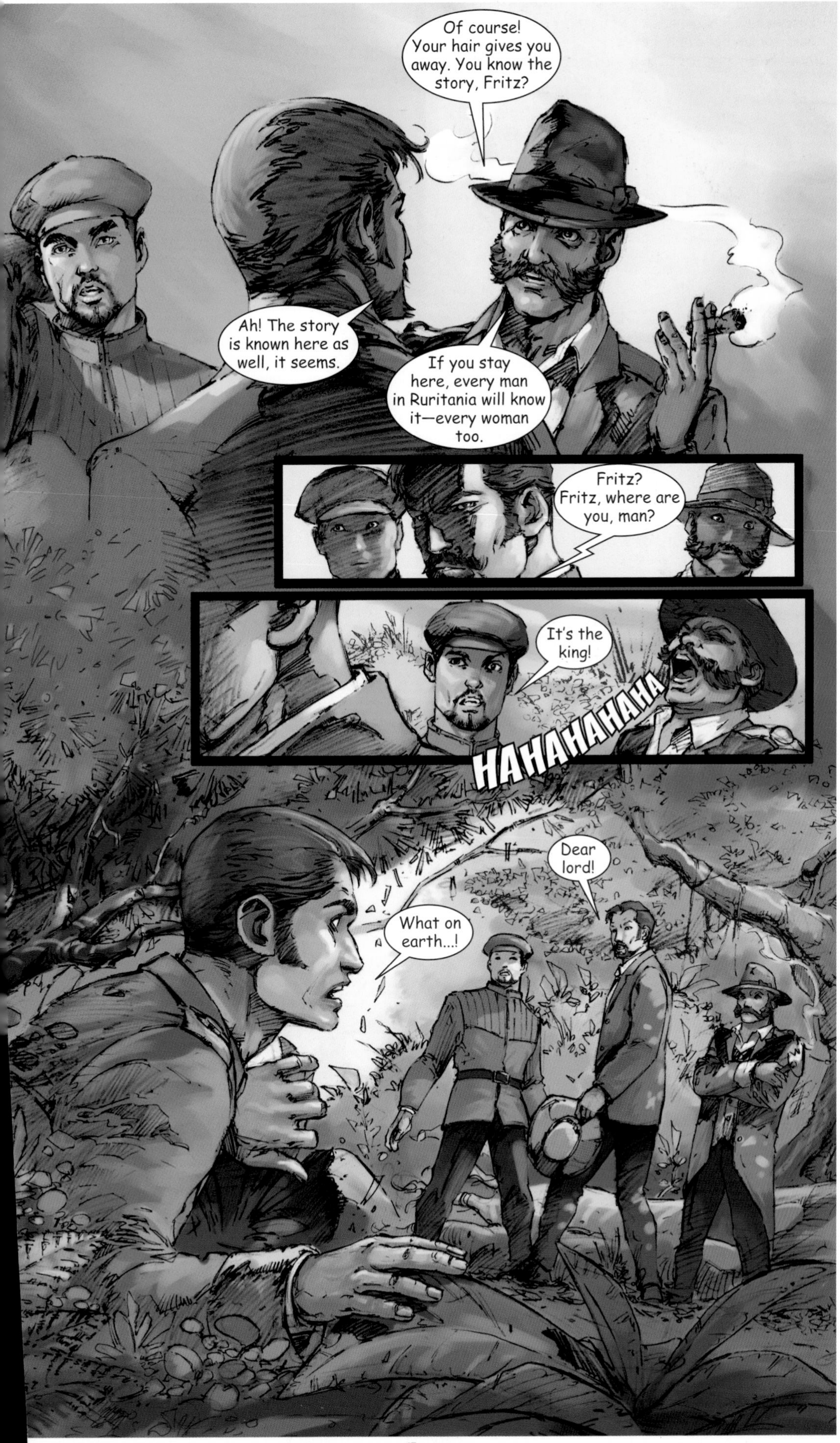
Of course! Your hair gives you away. You know the story, Fritz?
Ah! The story is known here as well, it seems.
If you stay here, every man in Ruritania will know it—every woman too.
Fritz? Fritz, where are you, man?
It's the king!
HAHAHAHAHA
Dear lord!
What on earth...!

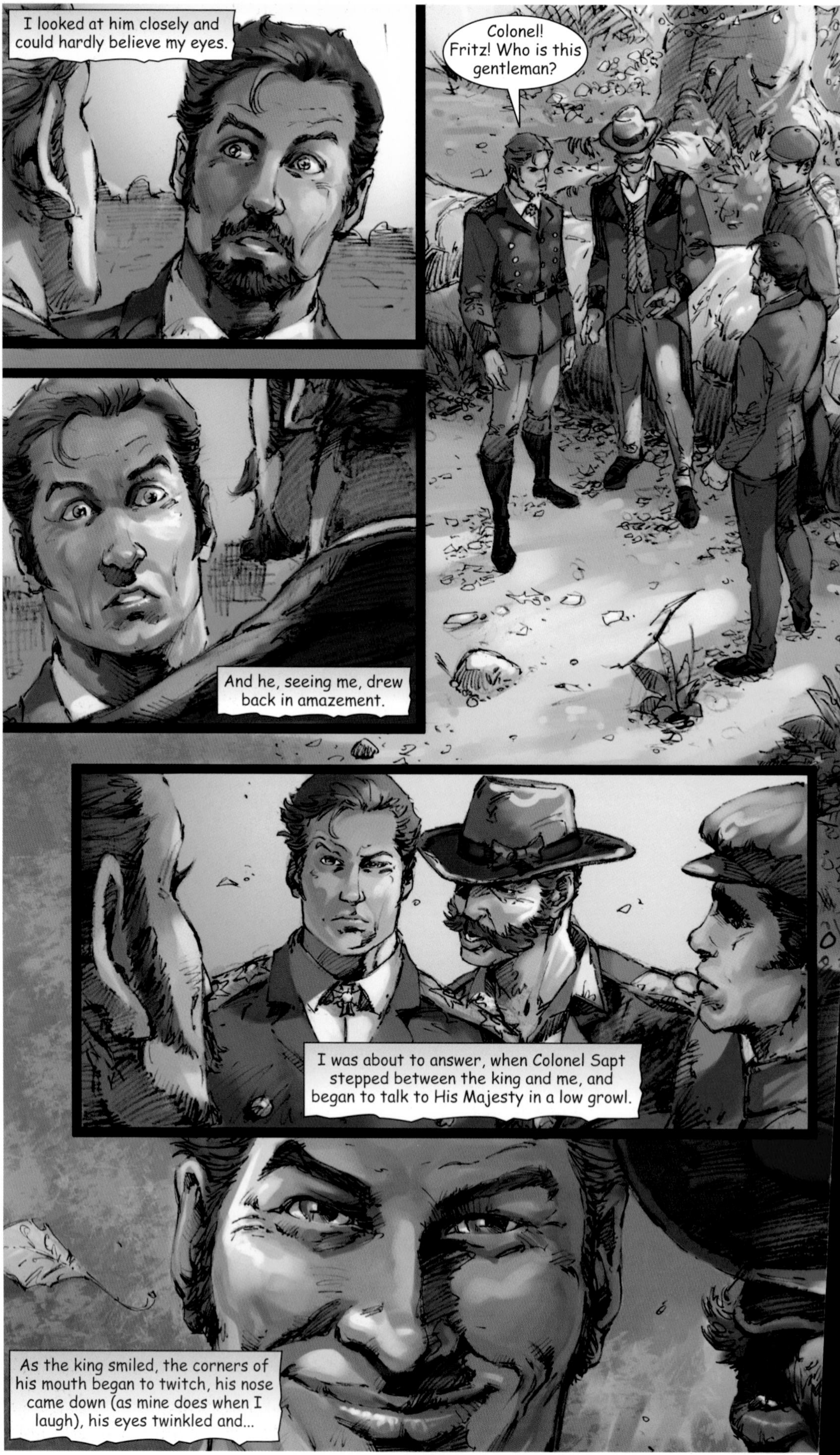
I looked at him closely and could hardly believe my eyes.
Colonel! Fritz! Who is this gentleman?
And he, seeing me, drew back in amazement.
I was about to answer, when Colonel Sapt stepped between the king and me, and began to talk to His Majesty in a low growl.
As the king smiled, the corners of his mouth began to twitch, his nose came down (as mine does when I laugh), his eyes twinkled and...

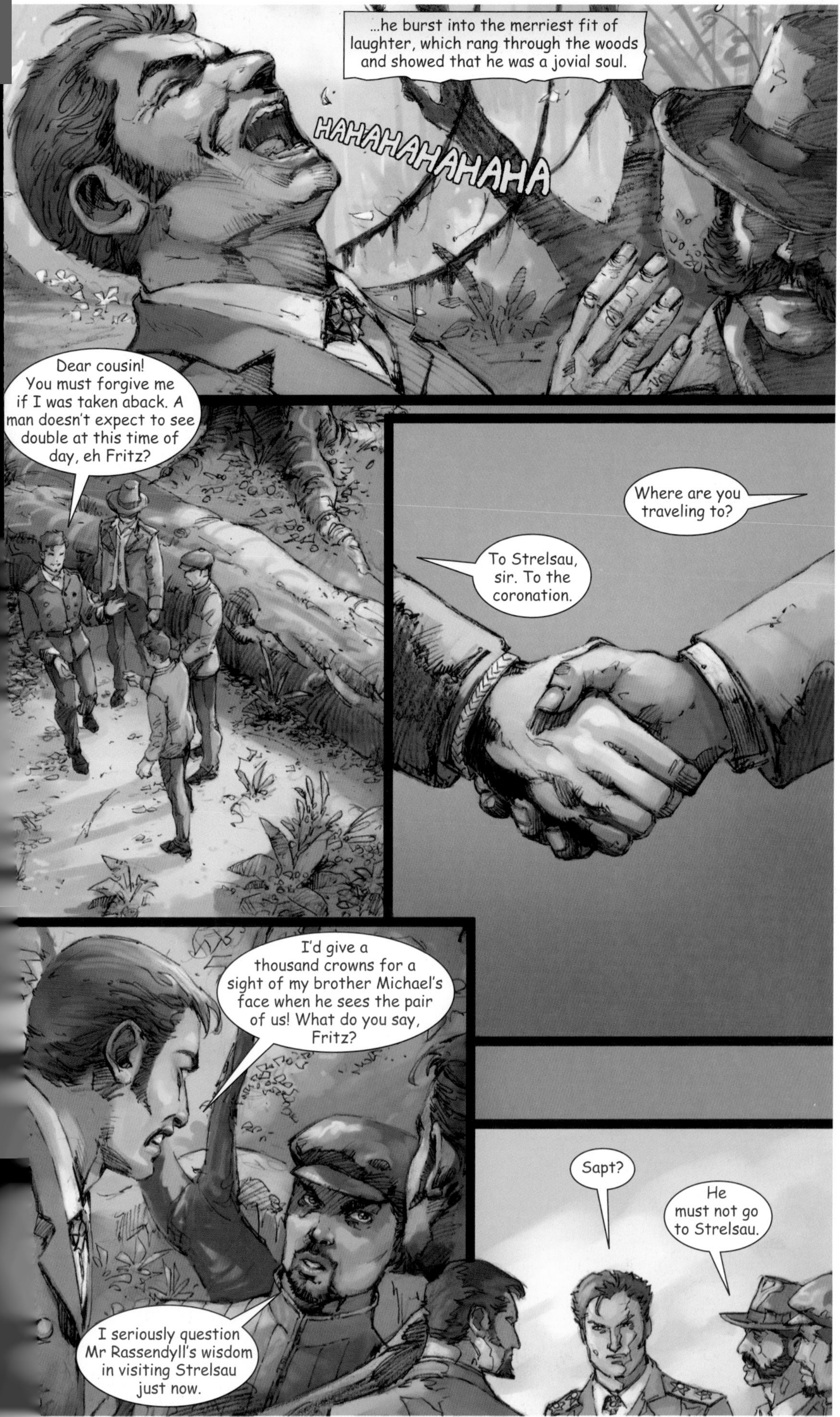
...he burst into the merriest fit of laughter, which rang through the woods and showed that he was a jovial soul.
HAHAHAHAHAHAHA
Dear cousin! You must forgive me if I was taken aback. A man doesn't expect to see double at this time of day, eh Fritz?
Where are you traveling to?
To Strelsau, sir. To the coronation.
I'd give a thousand crowns for a sight of my brother Michael's face when he sees the pair of us! What do you say, Fritz?
I seriously question Mr Rassendyll's wisdom in visiting Strelsau just now.
Sapt?
He must not go to Strelsau.

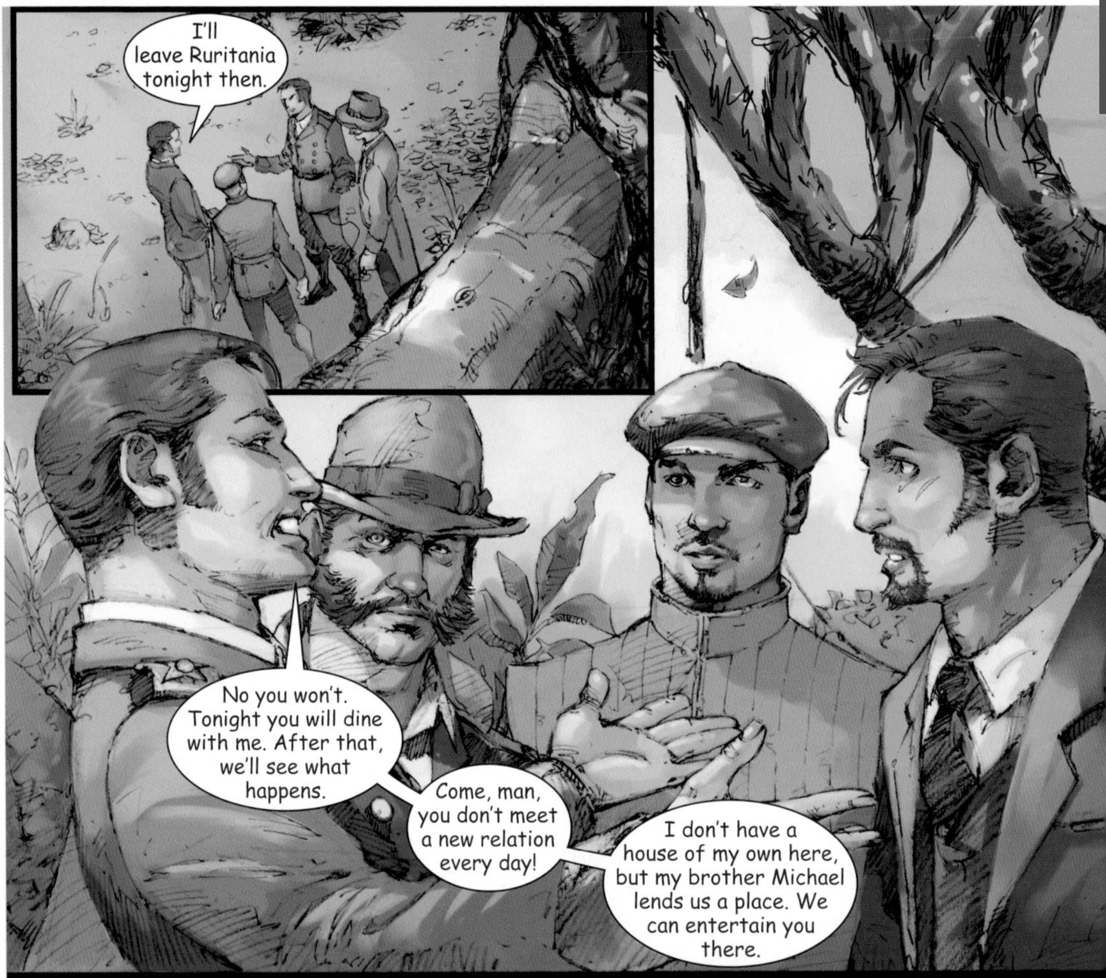
I'll leave Ruritania tonight then.
No you won't. Tonight you will dine with me. After that, we'll see what happens.
Come, man, you don't meet a new relation every day!
I don't have a house of my own here, but my brother Michael lends us a place. We can entertain you there.

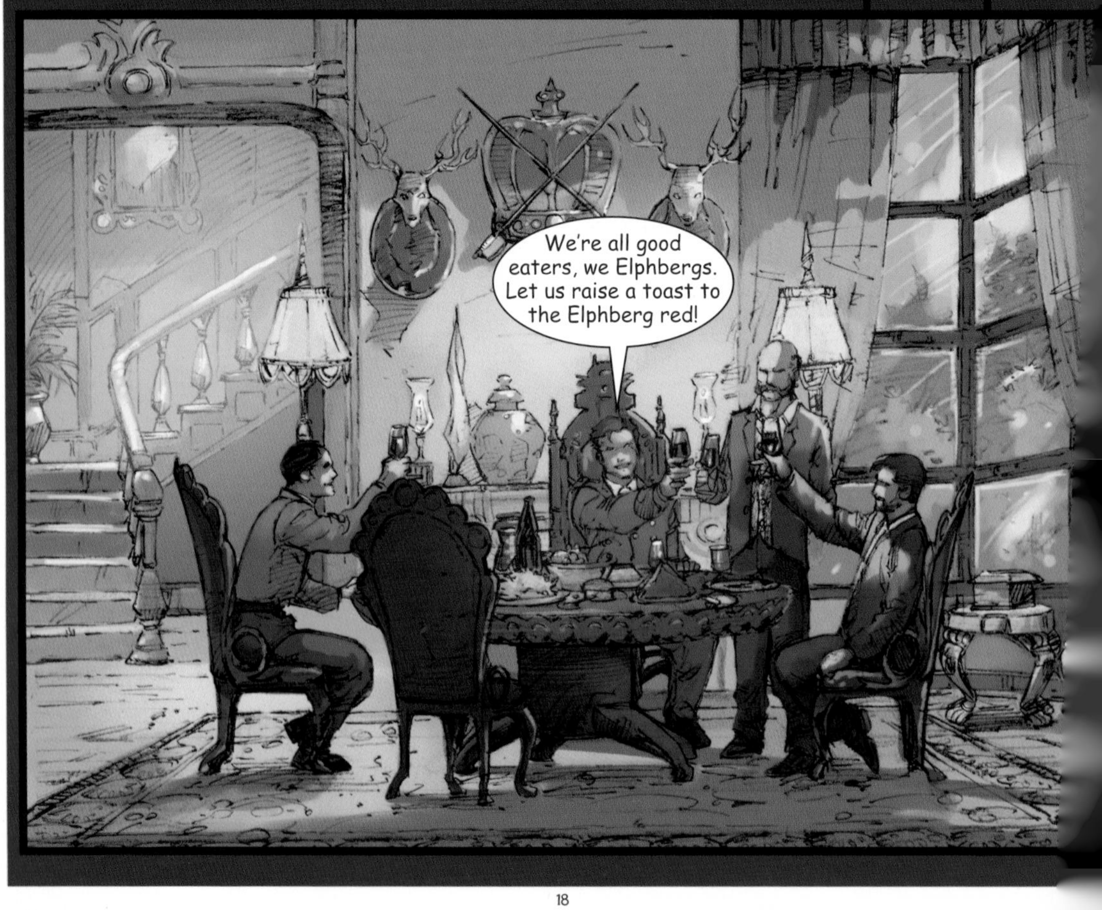
We're all good eaters, we Elphbergs. Let us raise a toast to the Elphberg red!

Remember you have to rise early tomorrow, Your Majesty.

But the king was only interested in enjoying himself, so we drank and talked and drank again.

Wine, Josef! Wine, man!

Remember tomorrow!

We have to leave for the coronation at six o'clock.

Yes, tomorrow! Let tomorrow take care of itself.

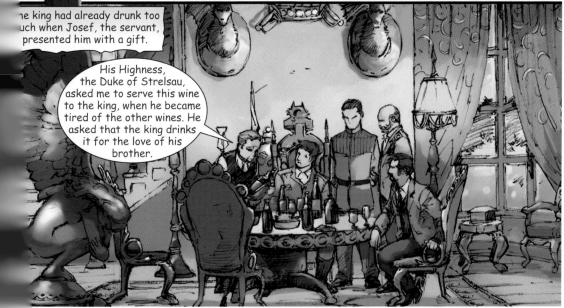

The king had already drunk too much when Josef, the servant, presented him with a gift.

His Highness, the Duke of Strelsau, asked me to serve this wine to the king, when he became tired of the other wines. He asked that the king drinks it for the love of his brother.

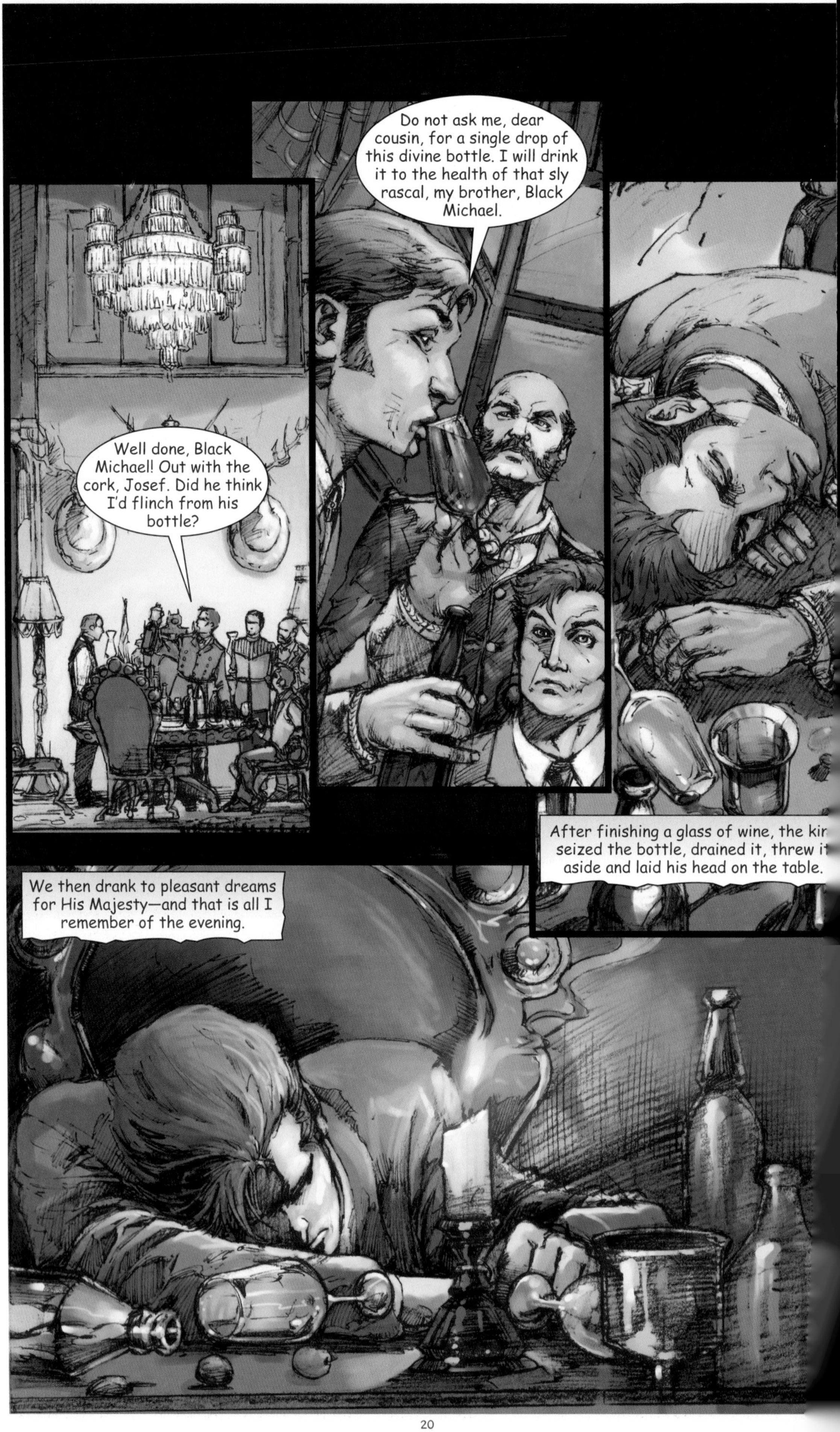

Well done, Black Michael! Out with the cork, Josef. Did he think I'd flinch from his bottle?
Do not ask me, dear cousin, for a single drop of this divine bottle. I will drink it to the health of that sly rascal, my brother, Black Michael.
After finishing a glass of wine, the ki
seized the bottle, drained it, threw i
aside and laid his head on the table.
We then drank to pleasant dreams for His Majesty—and that is all I remember of the evening.

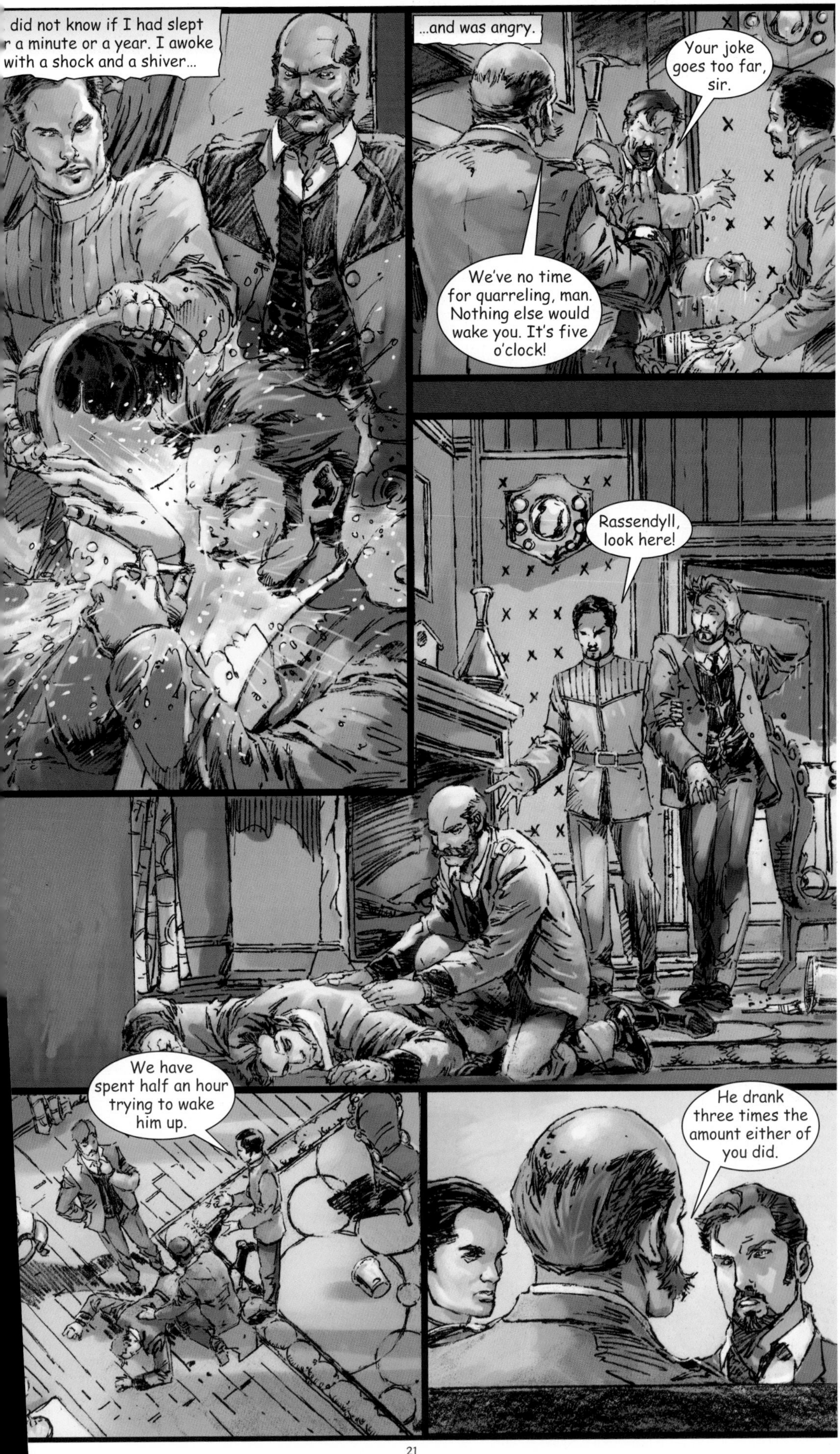

did not know if I had slept
r a minute or a year. I awoke
with a shock and a shiver...
...and was angry.
Your joke goes too far, sir.
We've no time for quarreling, man. Nothing else would wake you. It's five o'clock!
Rassendyll, look here!
We have spent half an hour trying to wake him up.
He drank three times the amount either of you did.

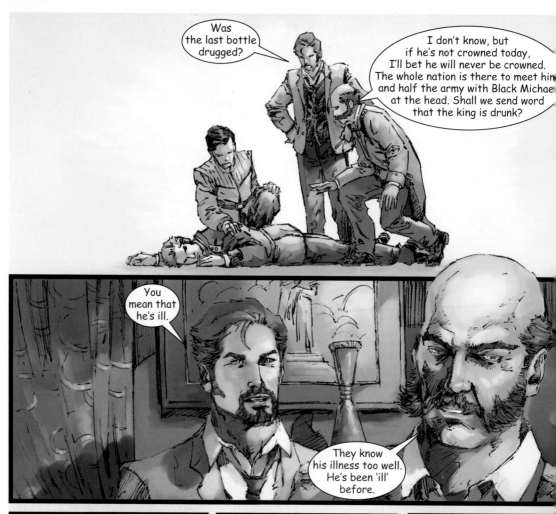

Was the last bottle drugged?

I don't know, but if he's not crowned today, I'll bet he will never be crowned. The whole nation is there to meet him and half the army with Black Michael at the head. Shall we send word that the king is drunk?

You mean that he's ill.

They know his illness too well. He's been 'ill' before.

Tell me, do you think the king was drugged?

I do.

And who drugged him?

That damned hound, Black Michael. He wants to be the king.

If he is not crowned in Strelsau today, Duke Michael will take his place as the new king.

As a man grows old, he believes in fate. Fate sent you here. And fate sends you to Strelsau now to take the place of the king!

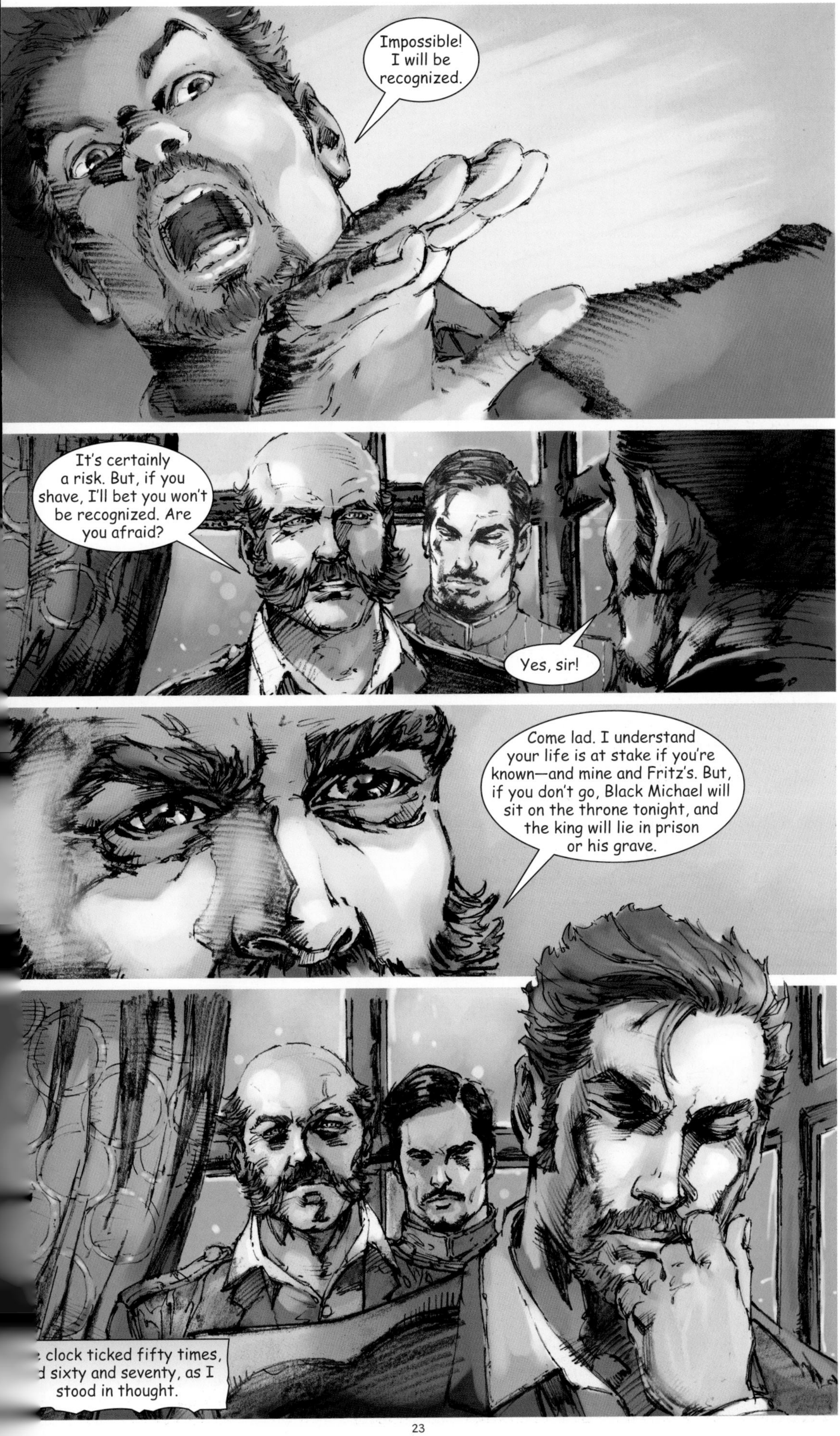

Impossible! I will be recognized.
It's certainly a risk. But, if you shave, I'll bet you won't be recognized. Are you afraid?
Yes, sir!
Come lad. I understand your life is at stake if you're known—and mine and Fritz's. But, if you don't go, Black Michael will sit on the throne tonight, and the king will lie in prison or his grave.
clock ticked fifty times,
d sixty and seventy, as I
stood in thought.

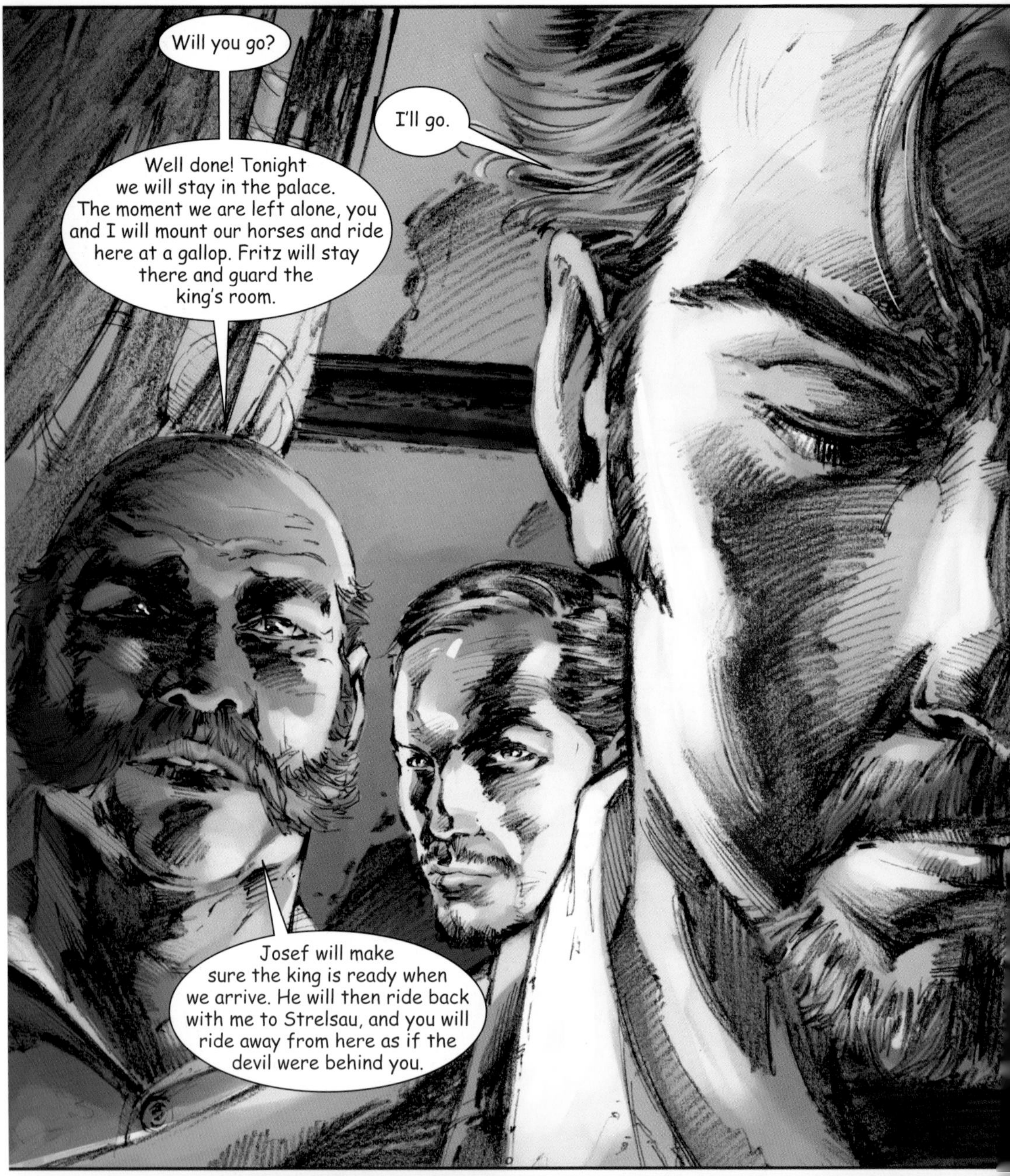
Will you go?
I'll go.
Well done! Tonight we will stay in the palace. The moment we are left alone, you and I will mount our horses and ride here at a gallop. Fritz will stay there and guard the king's room.
Josef will make sure the king is ready when we arrive. He will then ride back with me to Strelsau, and you will ride away from here as if the devil were behind you.

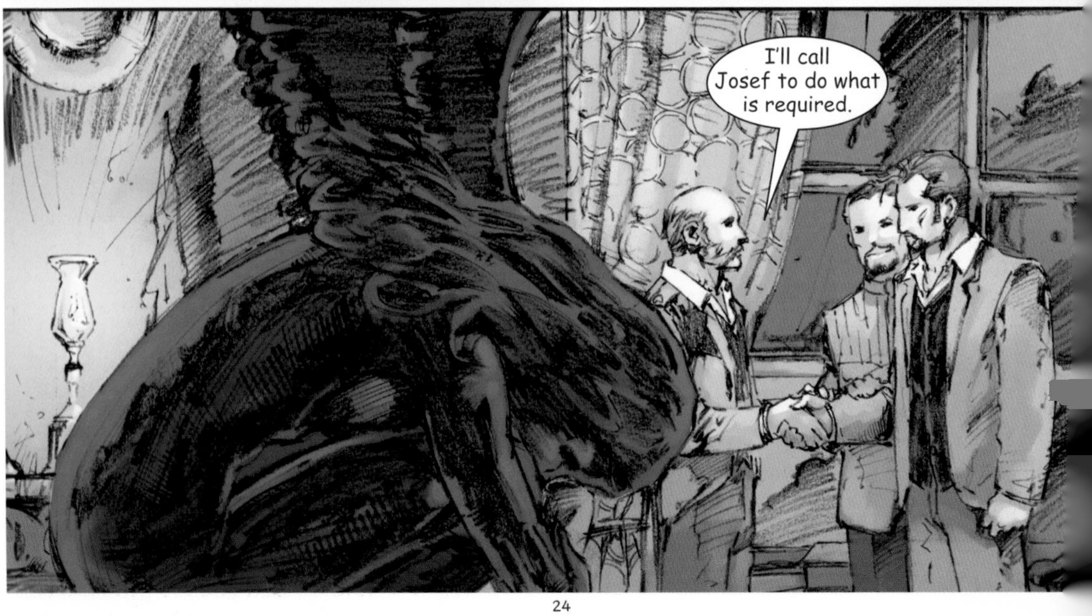
I'll call Josef to do what is required.

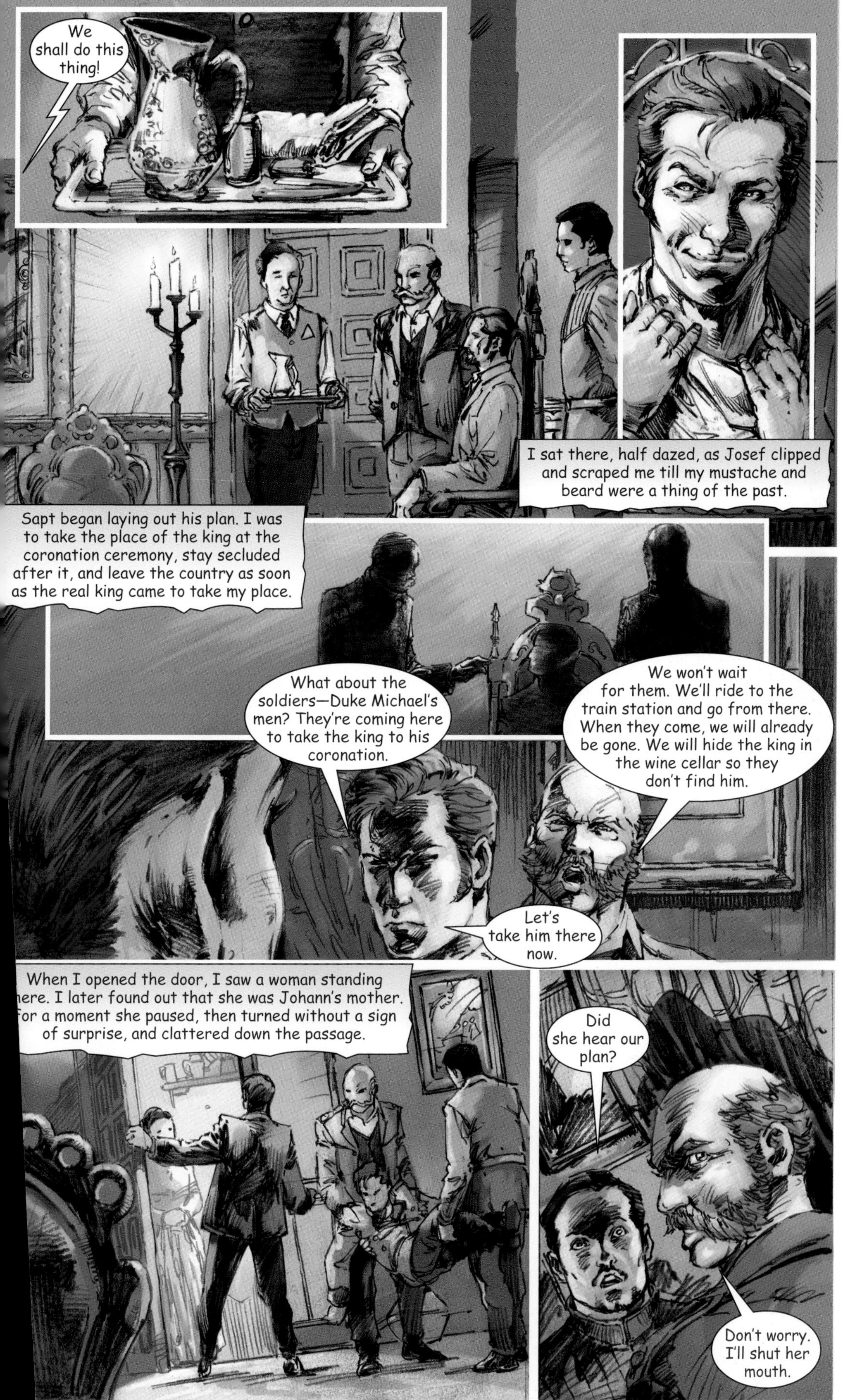
We shall do this thing!
I sat there, half dazed, as Josef clipped and scraped me till my mustache and beard were a thing of the past.
Sapt began laying out his plan. I was to take the place of the king at the coronation ceremony, stay secluded after it, and leave the country as soon as the real king came to take my place.
What about the soldiers—Duke Michael's men? They're coming here to take the king to his coronation.
We won't wait for them. We'll ride to the train station and go from there. When they come, we will already be gone. We will hide the king in the wine cellar so they don't find him.
Let's take him there now.
When I opened the door, I saw a woman standing here. I later found out that she was Johann's mother. For a moment she paused, then turned without a sign of surprise, and clattered down the passage.
Did she hear our plan?
Don't worry. I'll shut her mouth.

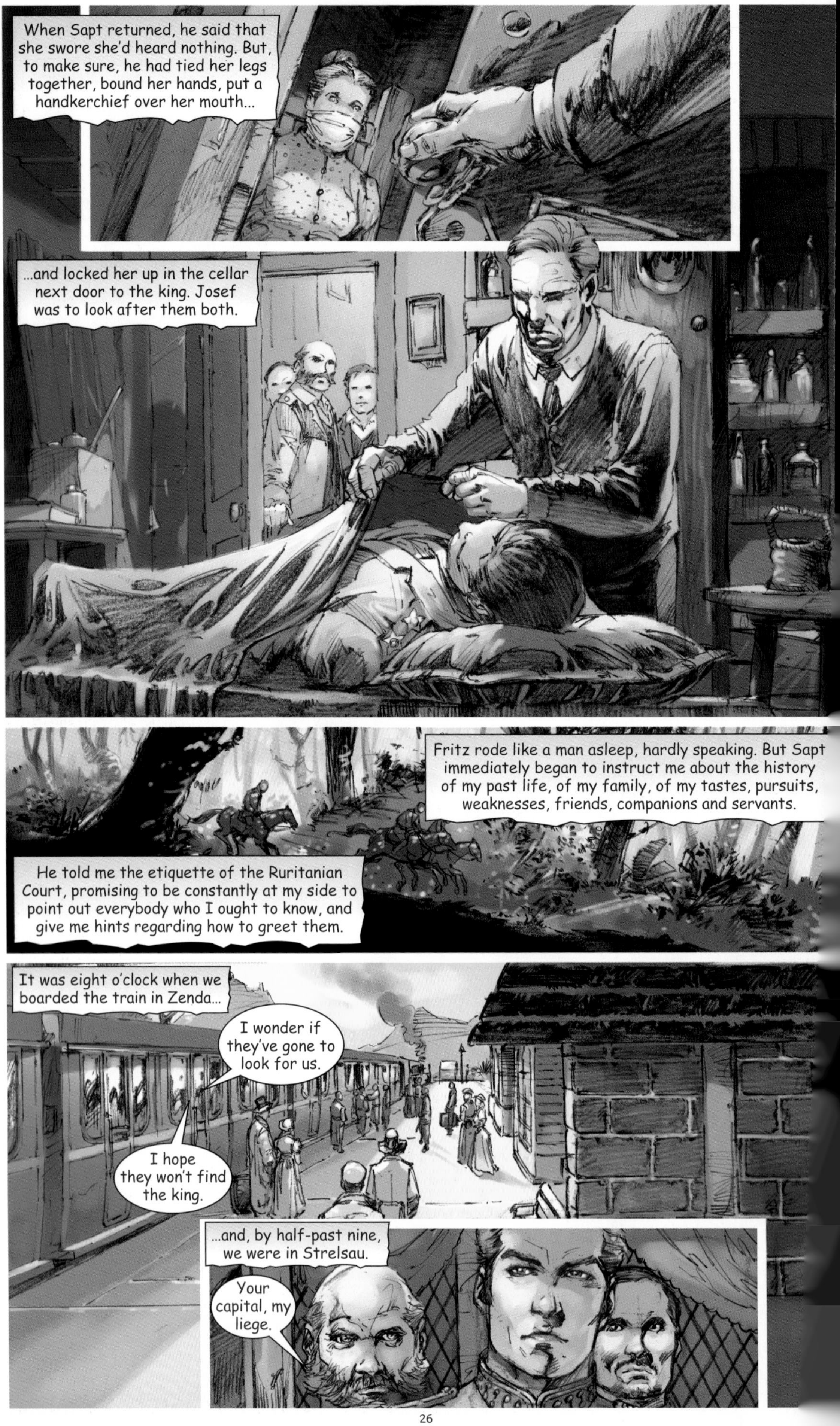

When Sapt returned, he said that she swore she'd heard nothing. But, to make sure, he had tied her legs together, bound her hands, put a handkerchief over her mouth...
...and locked her up in the cellar next door to the king. Josef was to look after them both.
Fritz rode like a man asleep, hardly speaking. But Sapt immediately began to instruct me about the history of my past life, of my family, of my tastes, pursuits, weaknesses, friends, companions and servants.
He told me the etiquette of the Ruritanian Court, promising to be constantly at my side to point out everybody who I ought to know, and give me hints regarding how to greet them.
It was eight o'clock when we boarded the train in Zenda...
I wonder if they've gone to look for us.
I hope they won't find the king.
...and, by half-past nine, we were in Strelsau.
Your capital, my liege.

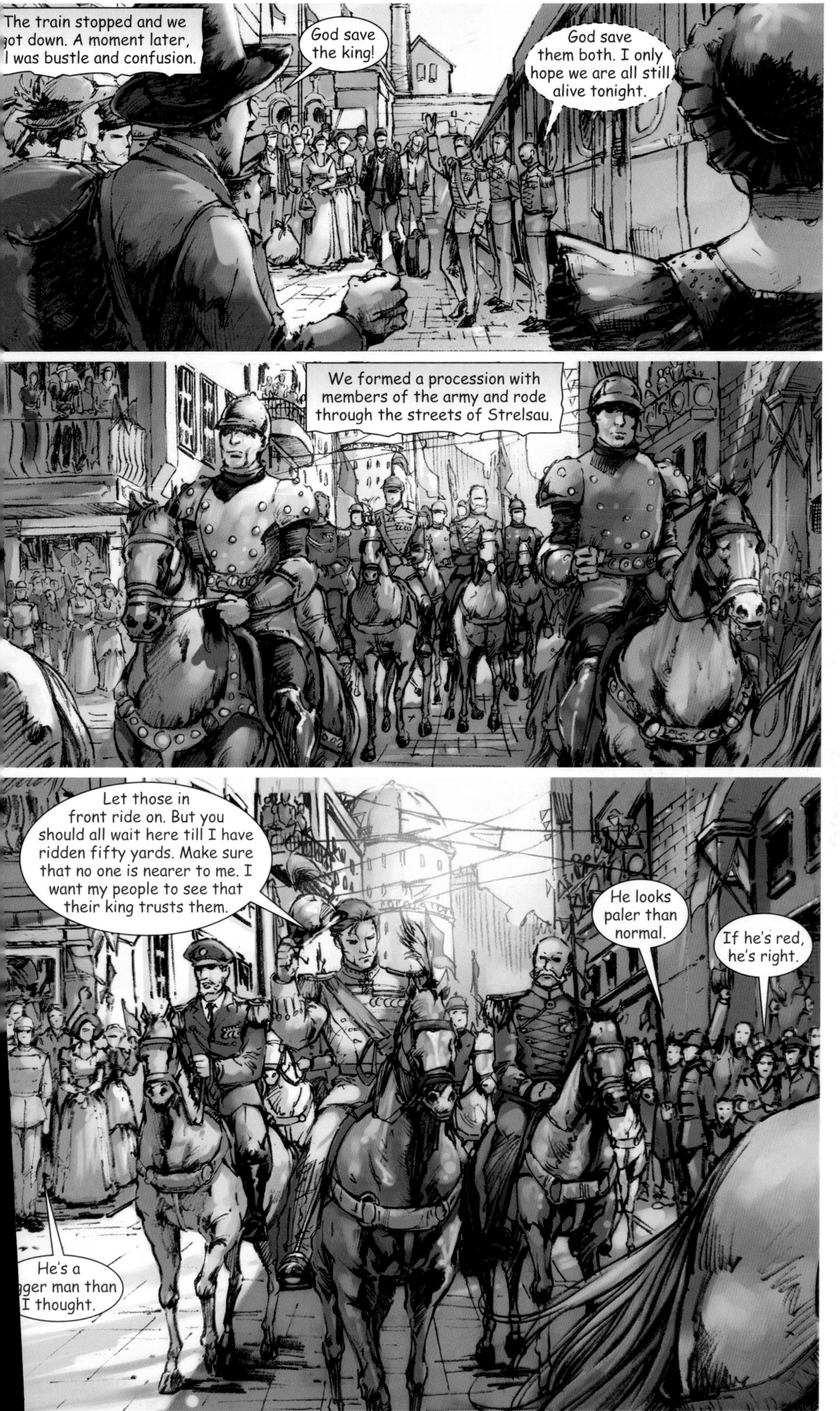
The train stopped and we got down. A moment later, all was bustle and confusion.
God save the king!
God save them both. I only hope we are all still alive tonight.
We formed a procession with members of the army and rode through the streets of Strelsau.
Let those in front ride on. But you should all wait here till I have ridden fifty yards. Make sure that no one is nearer to me. I want my people to see that their king trusts them.
He looks paler than normal.
If he's red, he's right.
He's a ...gger man than I thought.

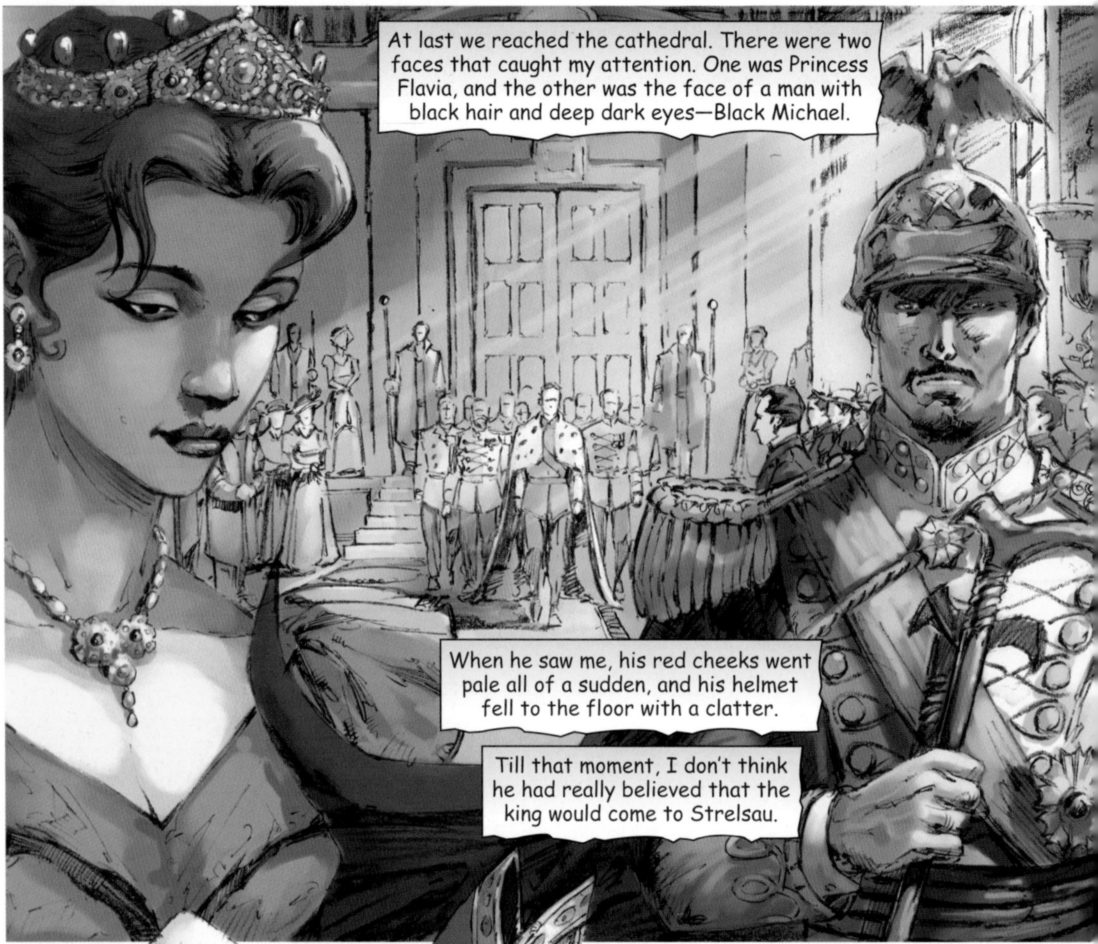
At last we reached the cathedral. There were two faces that caught my attention. One was Princess Flavia, and the other was the face of a man with black hair and deep dark eyes—Black Michael.
When he saw me, his red cheeks went pale all of a sudden, and his helmet fell to the floor with a clatter.
Till that moment, I don't think he had really believed that the king would come to Strelsau.

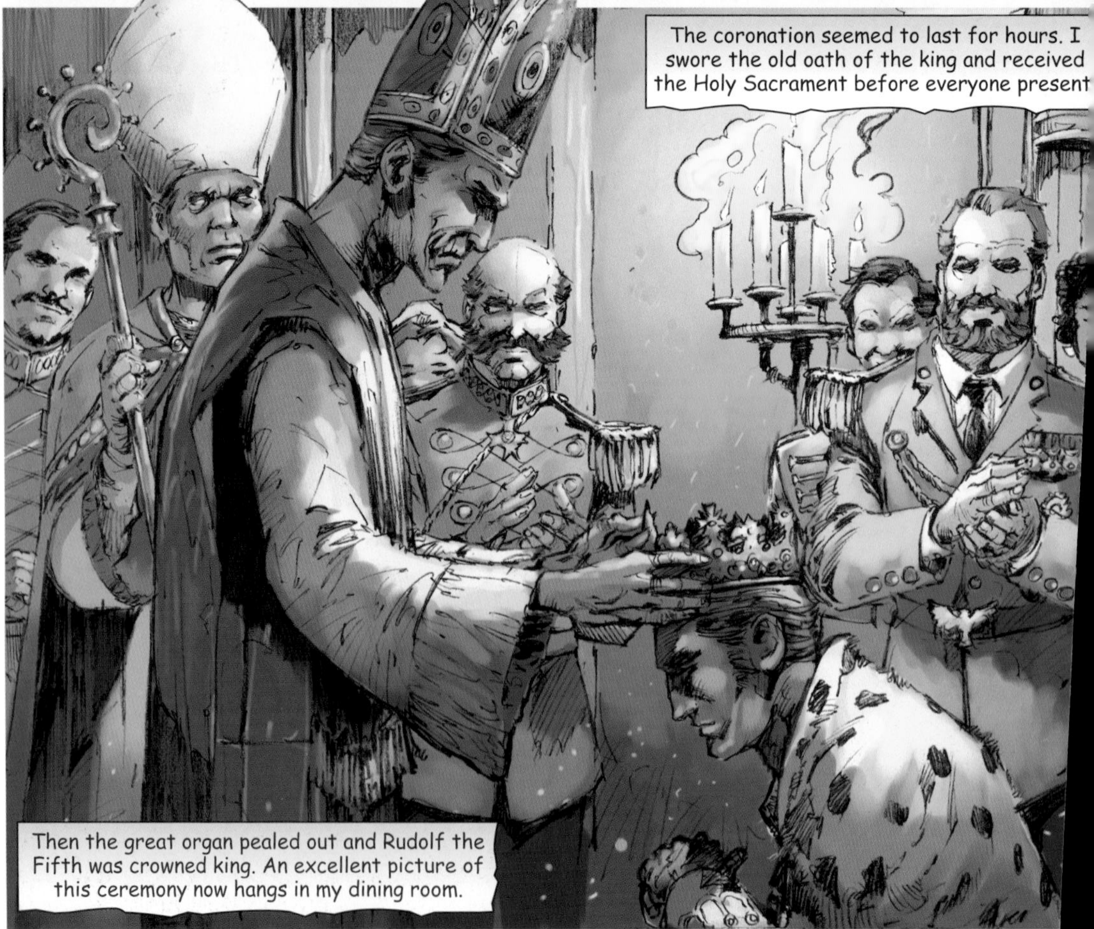
The coronation seemed to last for hours. I swore the old oath of the king and received the Holy Sacrament before everyone present
Then the great organ pealed out and Rudolf the Fifth was crowned king. An excellent picture of this ceremony now hangs in my dining room.

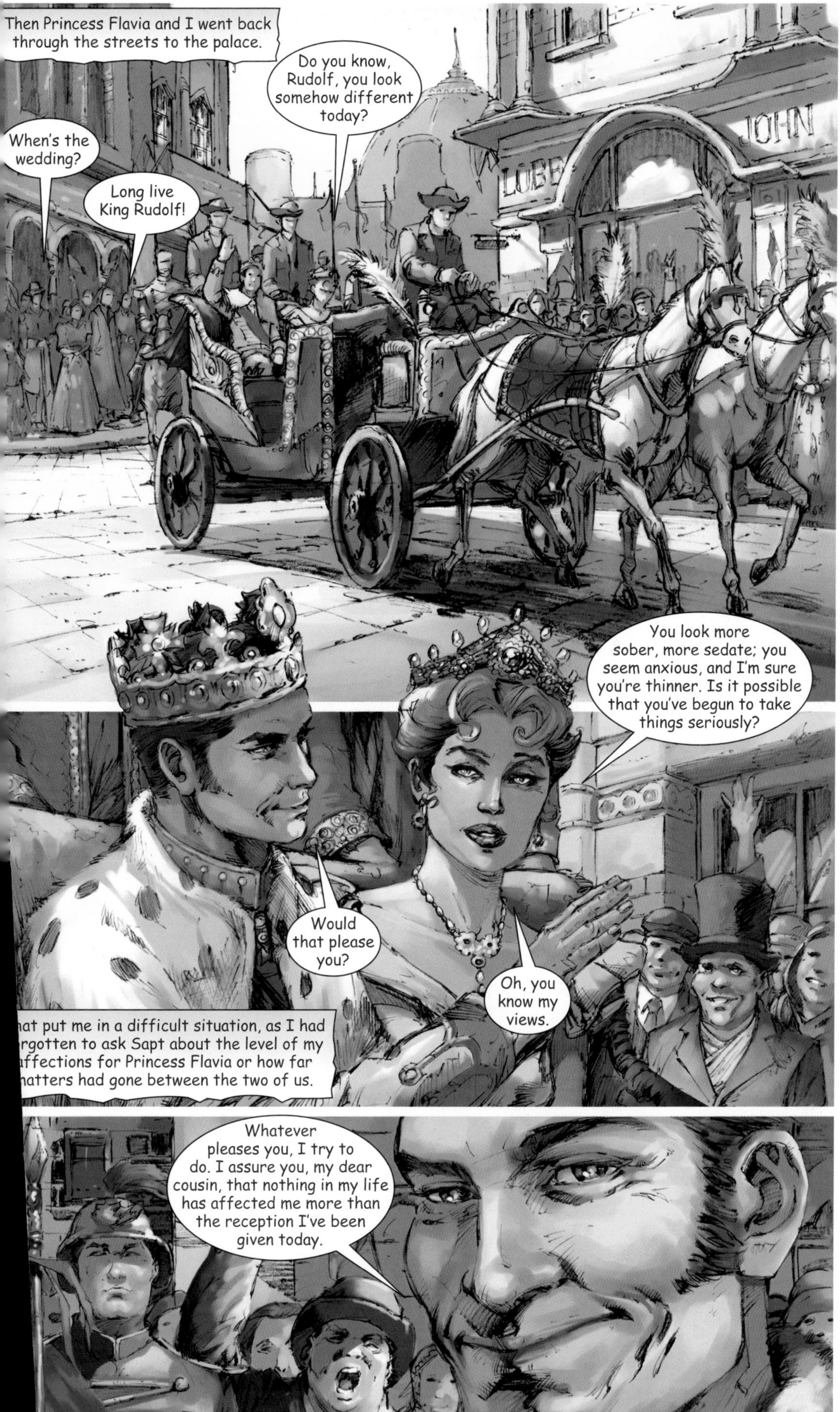

Then Princess Flavia and I went back through the streets to the palace.
When's the wedding?
Long live King Rudolf!
Do you know, Rudolf, you look somehow different today?
You look more sober, more sedate; you seem anxious, and I'm sure you're thinner. Is it possible that you've begun to take things seriously?
Would that please you?
Oh, you know my views.
hat put me in a difficult situation, as I had rgotten to ask Sapt about the level of my ffections for Princess Flavia or how far natters had gone between the two of us.
Whatever pleases you, I try to do. I assure you, my dear cousin, that nothing in my life has affected me more than the reception I've been given today.

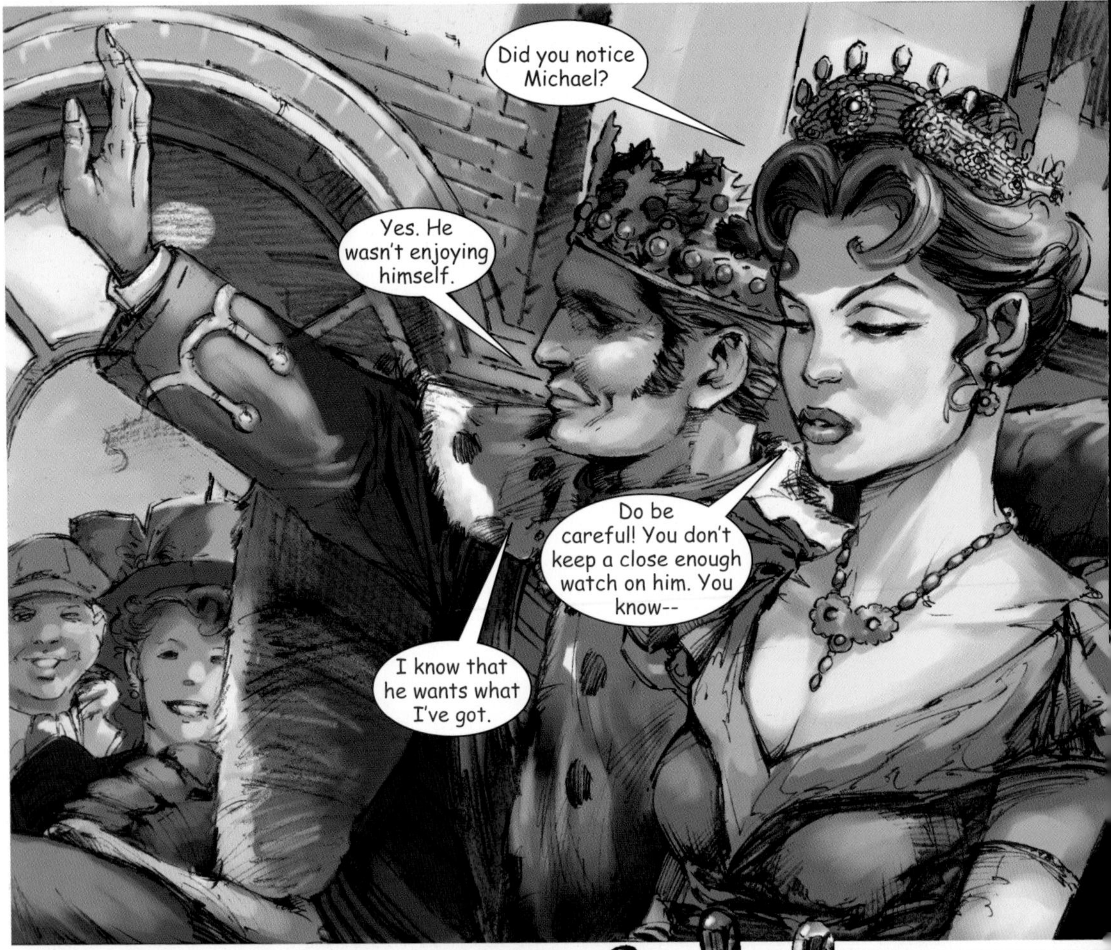
Did you notice Michael?
Yes. He wasn't enjoying himself.
Do be careful! You don't keep a close enough watch on him. You know--
I know that he wants what I've got.

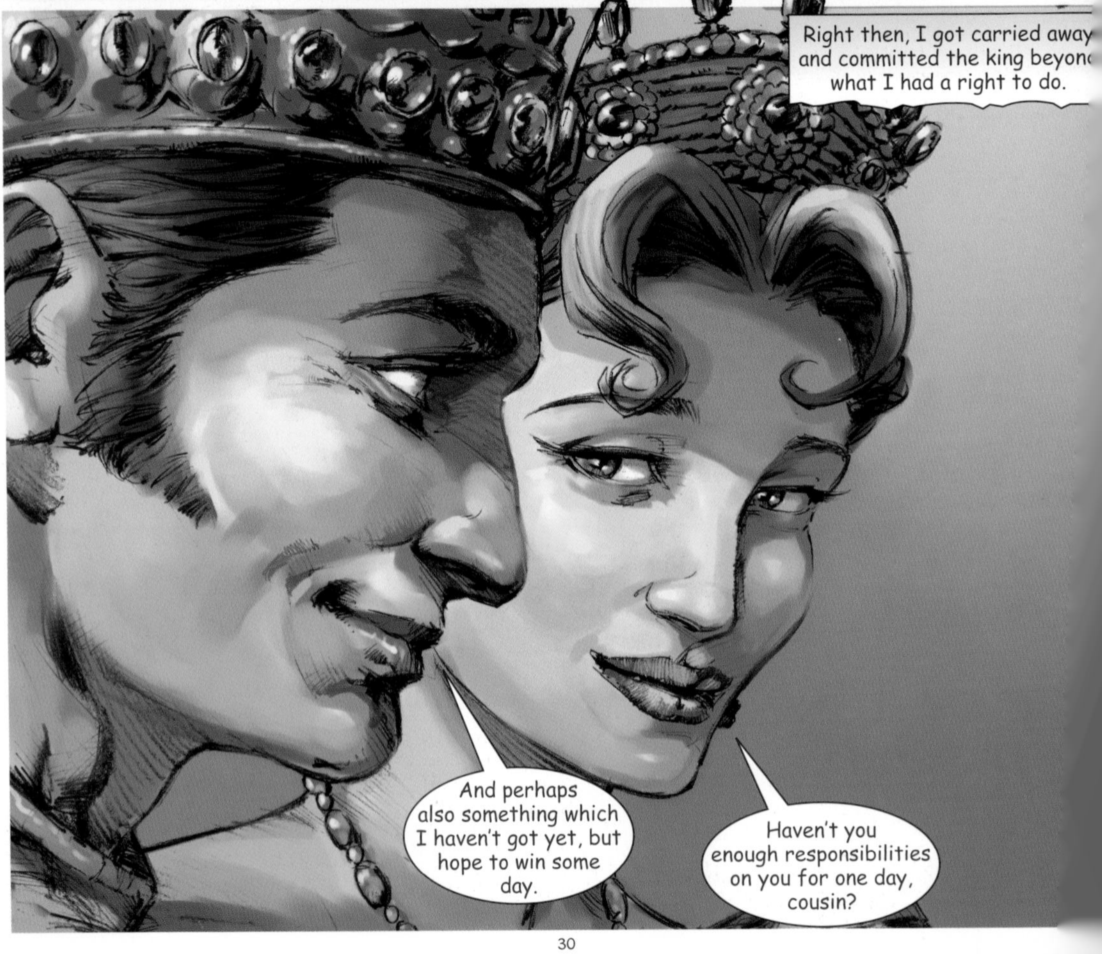
Right then, I got carried away and committed the king beyond what I had a right to do.
And perhaps also something which I haven't got yet, but hope to win some day.
Haven't you enough responsibilities on you for one day, cousin?

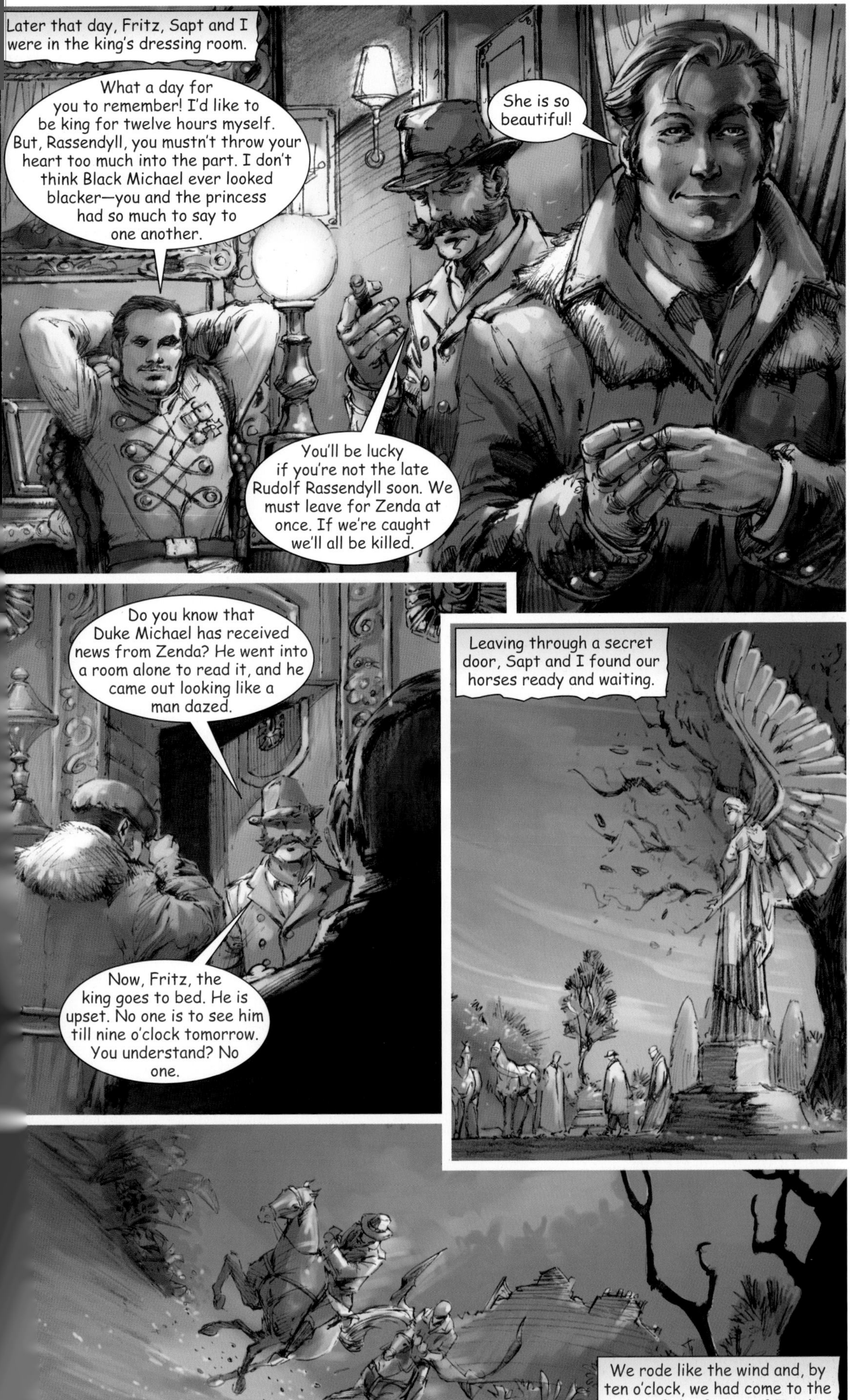
Later that day, Fritz, Sapt and I were in the king's dressing room.
What a day for you to remember! I'd like to be king for twelve hours myself. But, Rassendyll, you mustn't throw your heart too much into the part. I don't think Black Michael ever looked blacker—you and the princess had so much to say to one another.
She is so beautiful!
You'll be lucky if you're not the late Rudolf Rassendyll soon. We must leave for Zenda at once. If we're caught we'll all be killed.
Do you know that Duke Michael has received news from Zenda? He went into a room alone to read it, and he came out looking like a man dazed.
Now, Fritz, the king goes to bed. He is upset. No one is to see him till nine o'clock tomorrow. You understand? No one.
Leaving through a secret door, Sapt and I found our horses ready and waiting.
We rode like the wind and, by ten o'clock, we had come to the edge of the forest of Zenda.

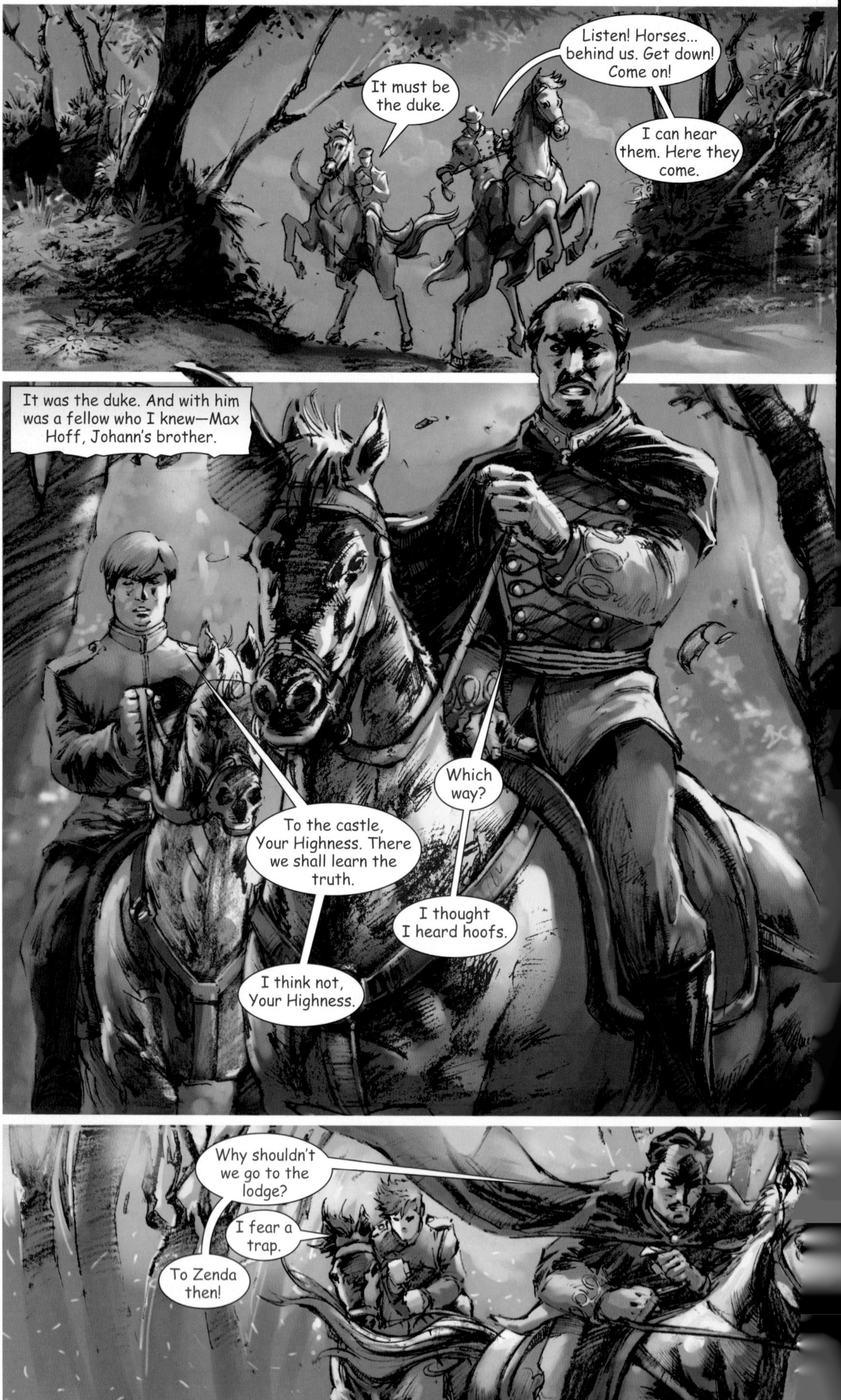
It must be the duke.
Listen! Horses... behind us. Get down! Come on!
I can hear them. Here they come.
It was the duke. And with him was a fellow who I knew—Max Hoff, Johann's brother.
Which way?
To the castle, Your Highness. There we shall learn the truth.
I thought I heard hoofs.
I think not, Your Highness.
Why shouldn't we go to the lodge?
I fear a trap.
To Zenda then!

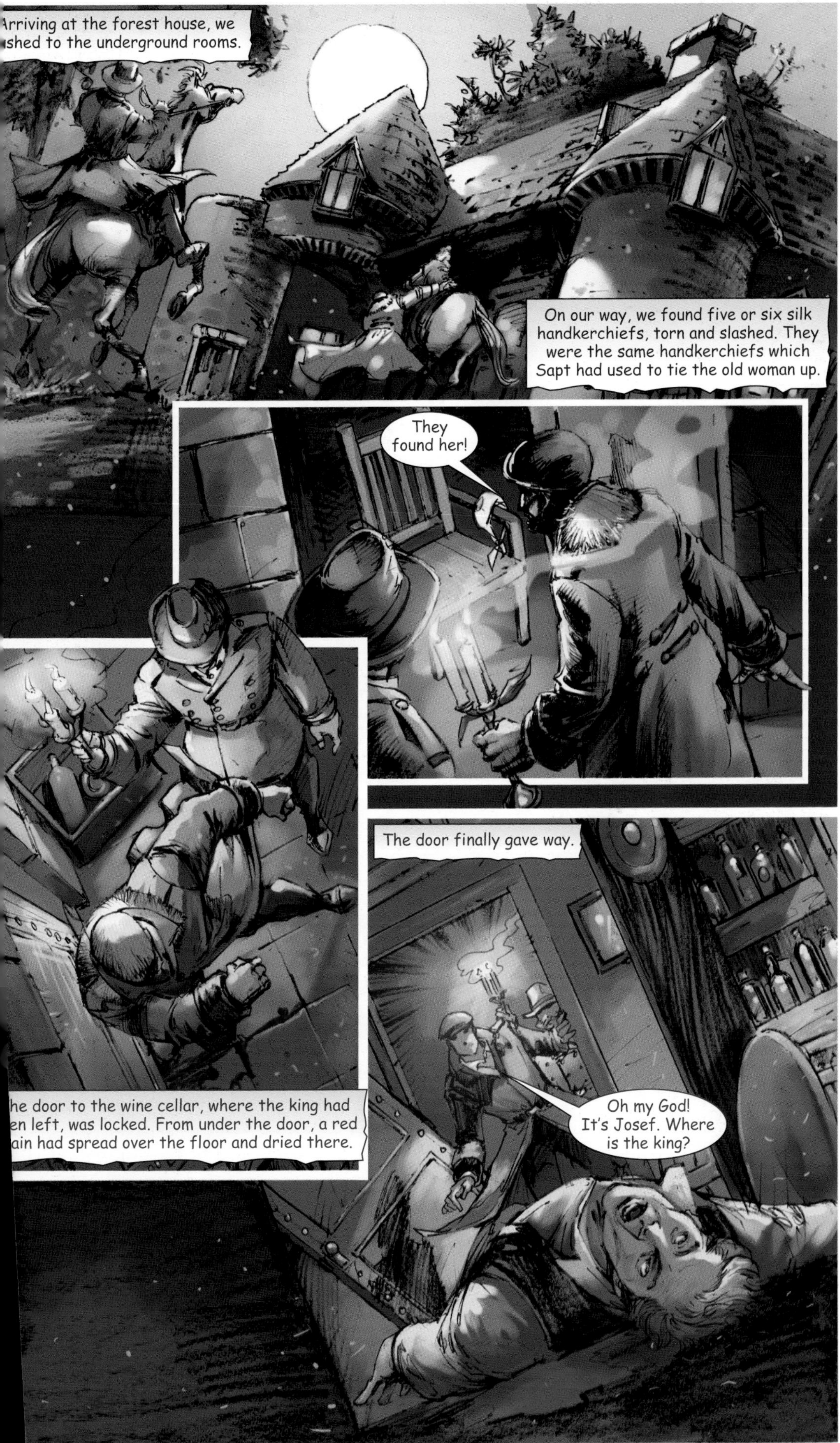
Arriving at the forest house, we
ished to the underground rooms.
On our way, we found five or six silk handkerchiefs, torn and slashed. They were the same handkerchiefs which Sapt had used to tie the old woman up.
They found her!
he door to the wine cellar, where the king had
en left, was locked. From under the door, a red
ain had spread over the floor and dried there.
The door finally gave way.
Oh my God! It's Josef. Where is the king?

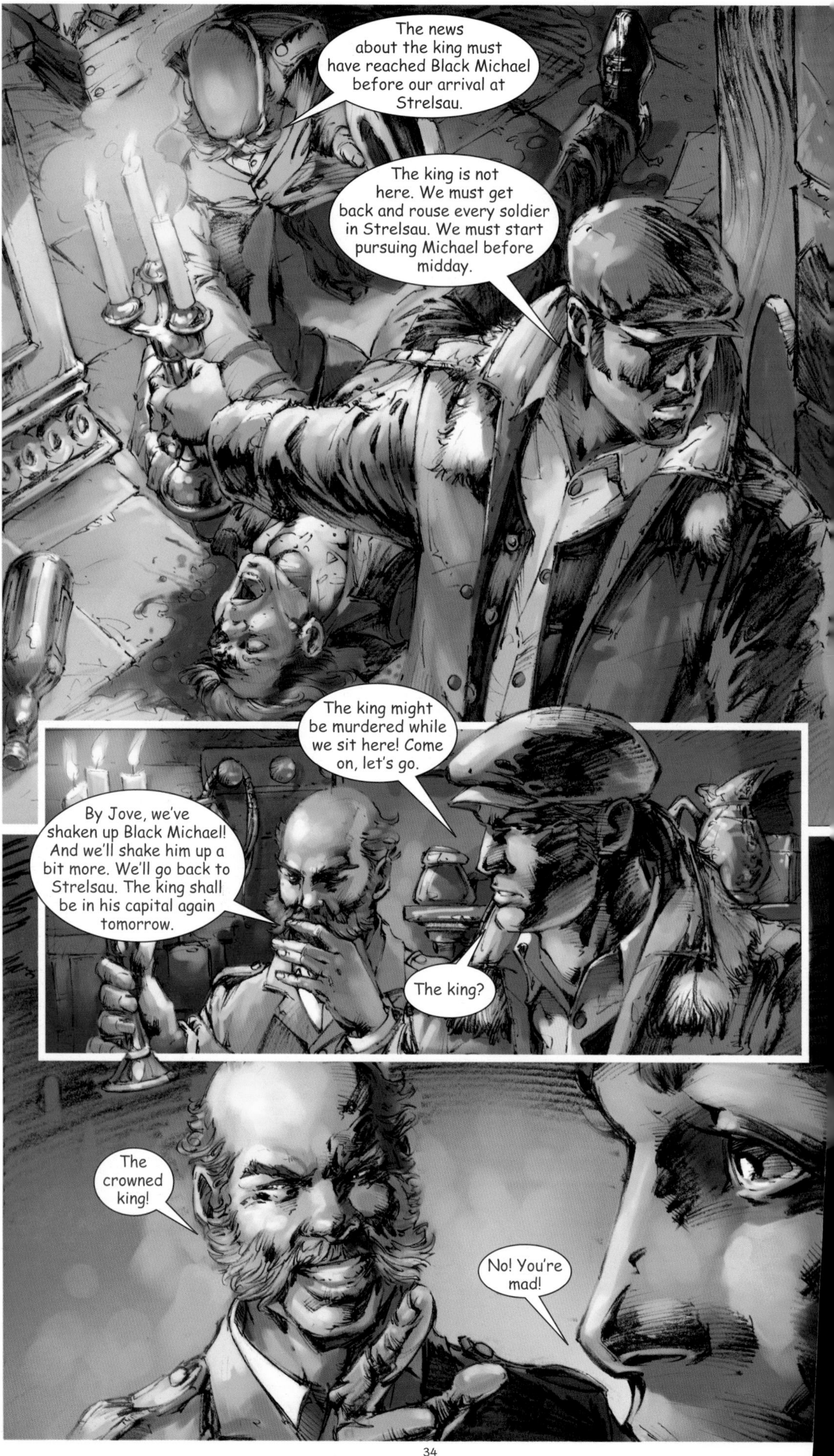
The news about the king must have reached Black Michael before our arrival at Strelsau.
The king is not here. We must get back and rouse every soldier in Strelsau. We must start pursuing Michael before midday.
The king might be murdered while we sit here! Come on, let's go.
By Jove, we've shaken up Black Michael! And we'll shake him up a bit more. We'll go back to Strelsau. The king shall be in his capital again tomorrow.
The king?
The crowned king!
No! You're mad!

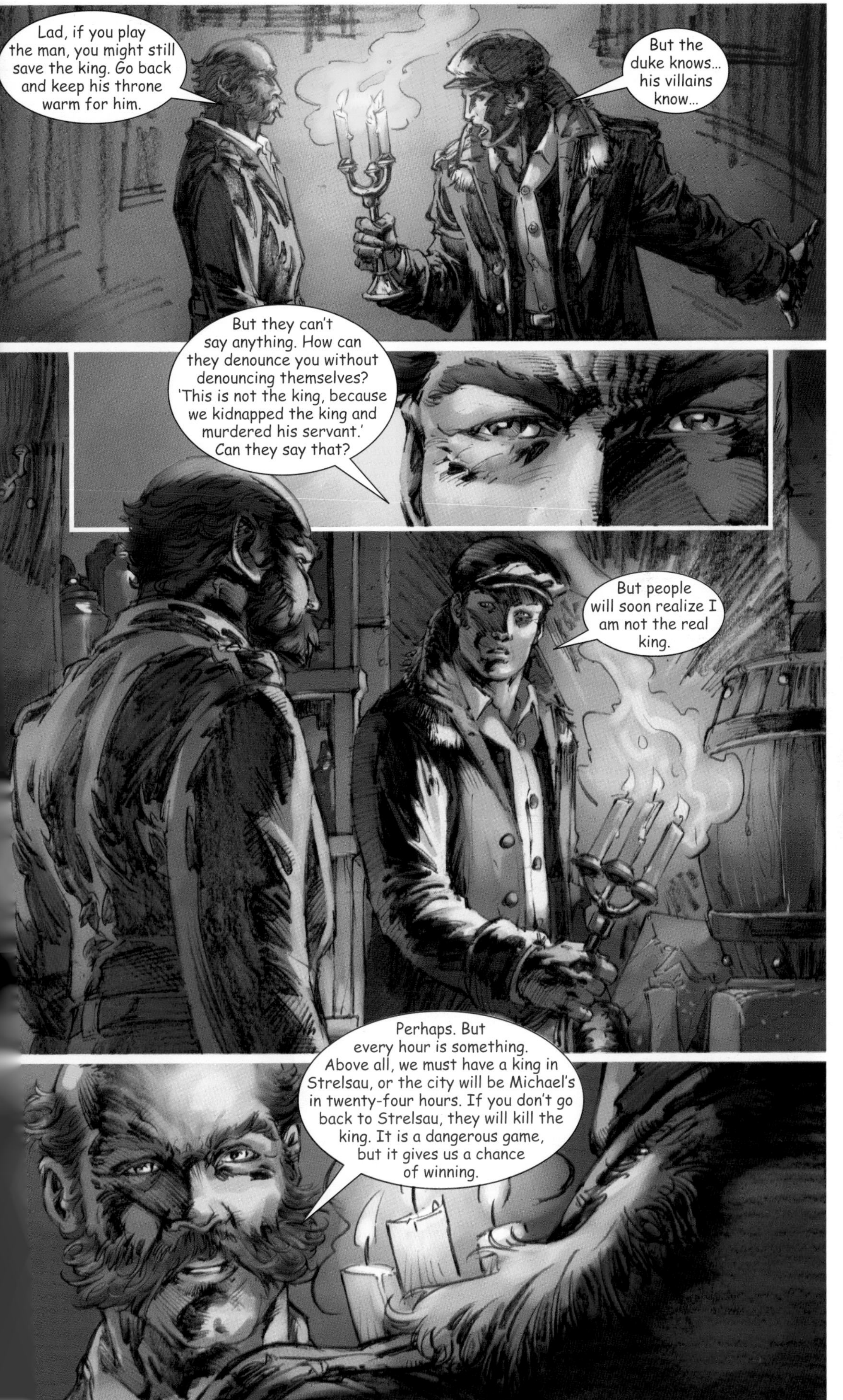

Lad, if you play the man, you might still save the king. Go back and keep his throne warm for him.
But the duke knows... his villains know...
But they can't say anything. How can they denounce you without denouncing themselves? 'This is not the king, because we kidnapped the king and murdered his servant.' Can they say that?
But people will soon realize I am not the real king.
Perhaps. But every hour is something. Above all, we must have a king in Strelsau, or the city will be Michael's in twenty-four hours. If you don't go back to Strelsau, they will kill the king. It is a dangerous game, but it gives us a chance of winning.

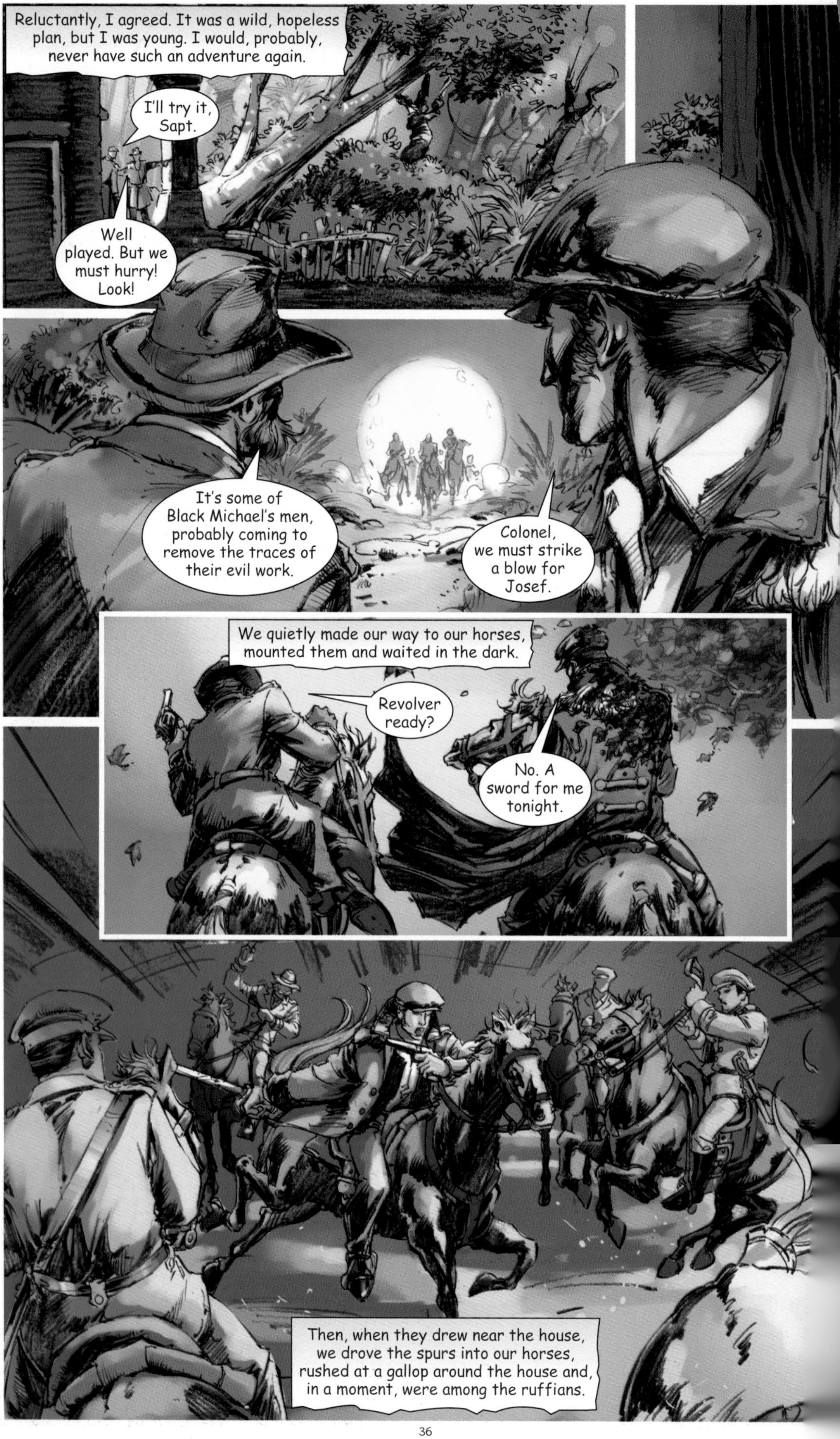

Reluctantly, I agreed. It was a wild, hopeless plan, but I was young. I would, probably, never have such an adventure again.
I'll try it, Sapt.
Well played. But we must hurry! Look!
It's some of Black Michael's men, probably coming to remove the traces of their evil work.
Colonel, we must strike a blow for Josef.
We quietly made our way to our horses, mounted them and waited in the dark.
Revolver ready?
No. A sword for me tonight.
Then, when they drew near the house, we drove the spurs into our horses, rushed at a gallop around the house and, in a moment, were among the ruffians.

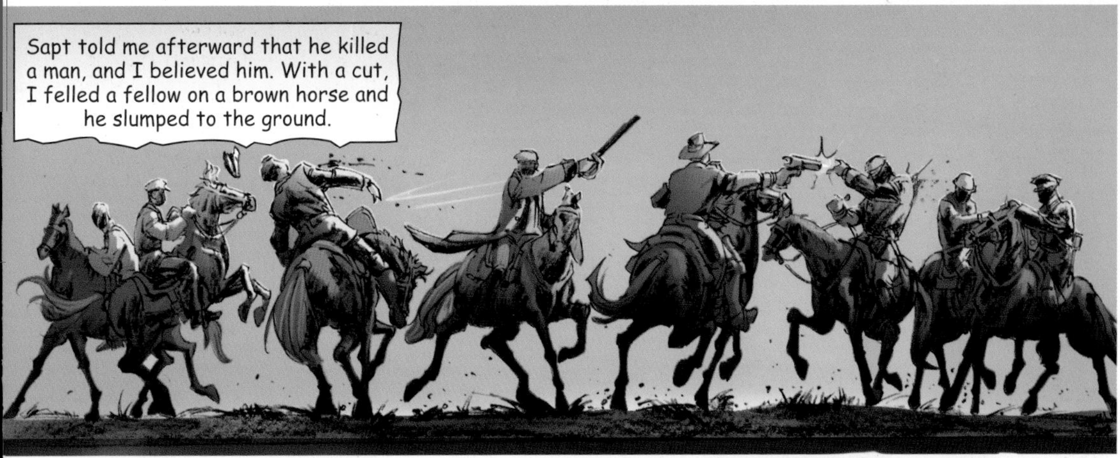
Sapt told me afterward that he killed a man, and I believed him. With a cut, I felled a fellow on a brown horse and he slumped to the ground.

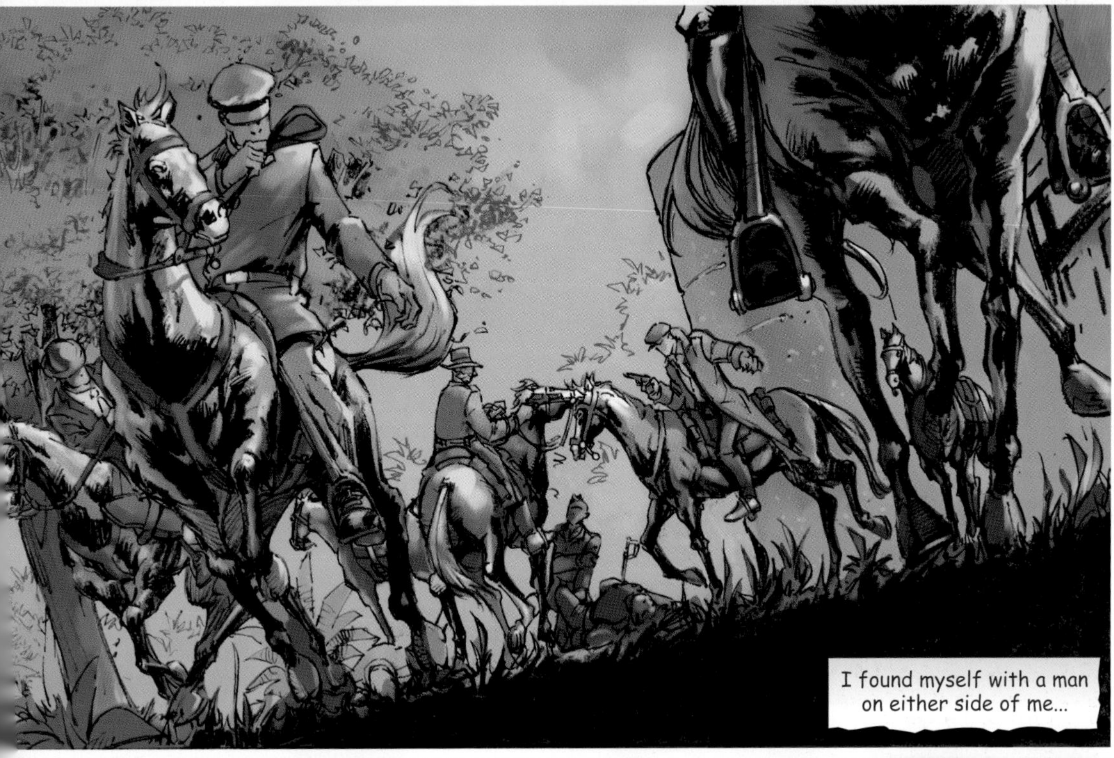
I found myself with a man on either side of me...

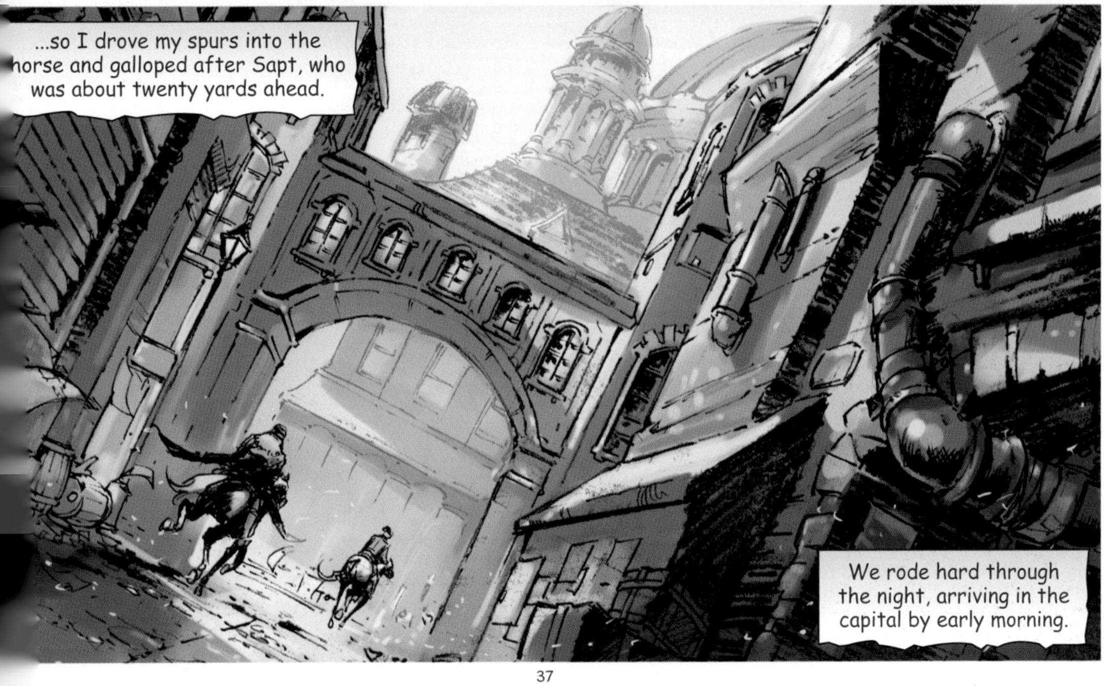
...so I drove my spurs into the horse and galloped after Sapt, who was about twenty yards ahead.
We rode hard through the night, arriving in the capital by early morning.

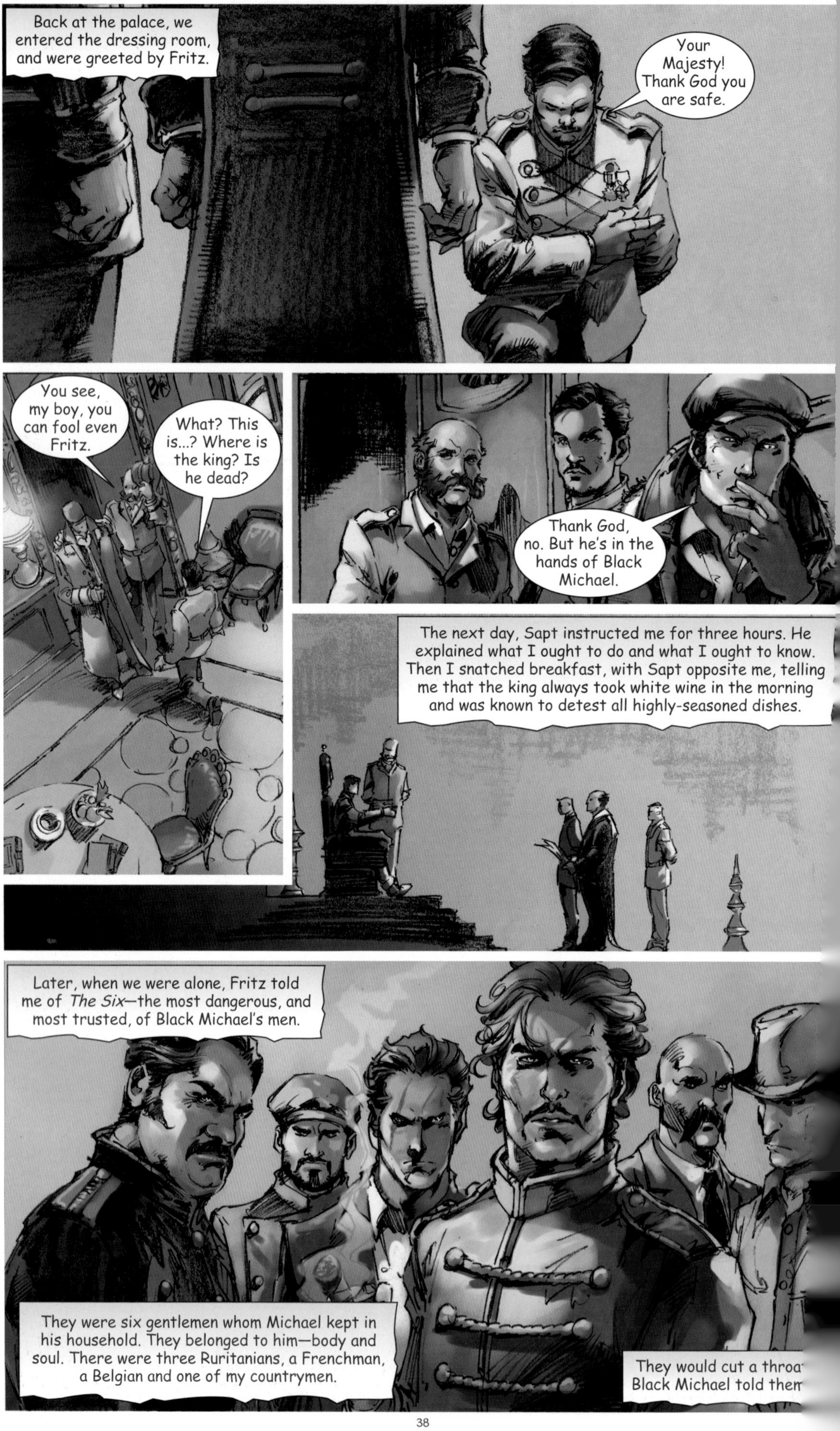
Back at the palace, we entered the dressing room, and were greeted by Fritz.
Your Majesty! Thank God you are safe.
You see, my boy, you can fool even Fritz.
What? This is...? Where is the king? Is he dead?
Thank God, no. But he's in the hands of Black Michael.
The next day, Sapt instructed me for three hours. He explained what I ought to do and what I ought to know. Then I snatched breakfast, with Sapt opposite me, telling me that the king always took white wine in the morning and was known to detest all highly-seasoned dishes.
Later, when we were alone, Fritz told me of *The Six*—the most dangerous, and most trusted, of Black Michael's men.
They were six gentlemen whom Michael kept in his household. They belonged to him—body and soul. There were three Ruritanians, a Frenchman, a Belgian and one of my countrymen.
They would cut a throa
Black Michael told them

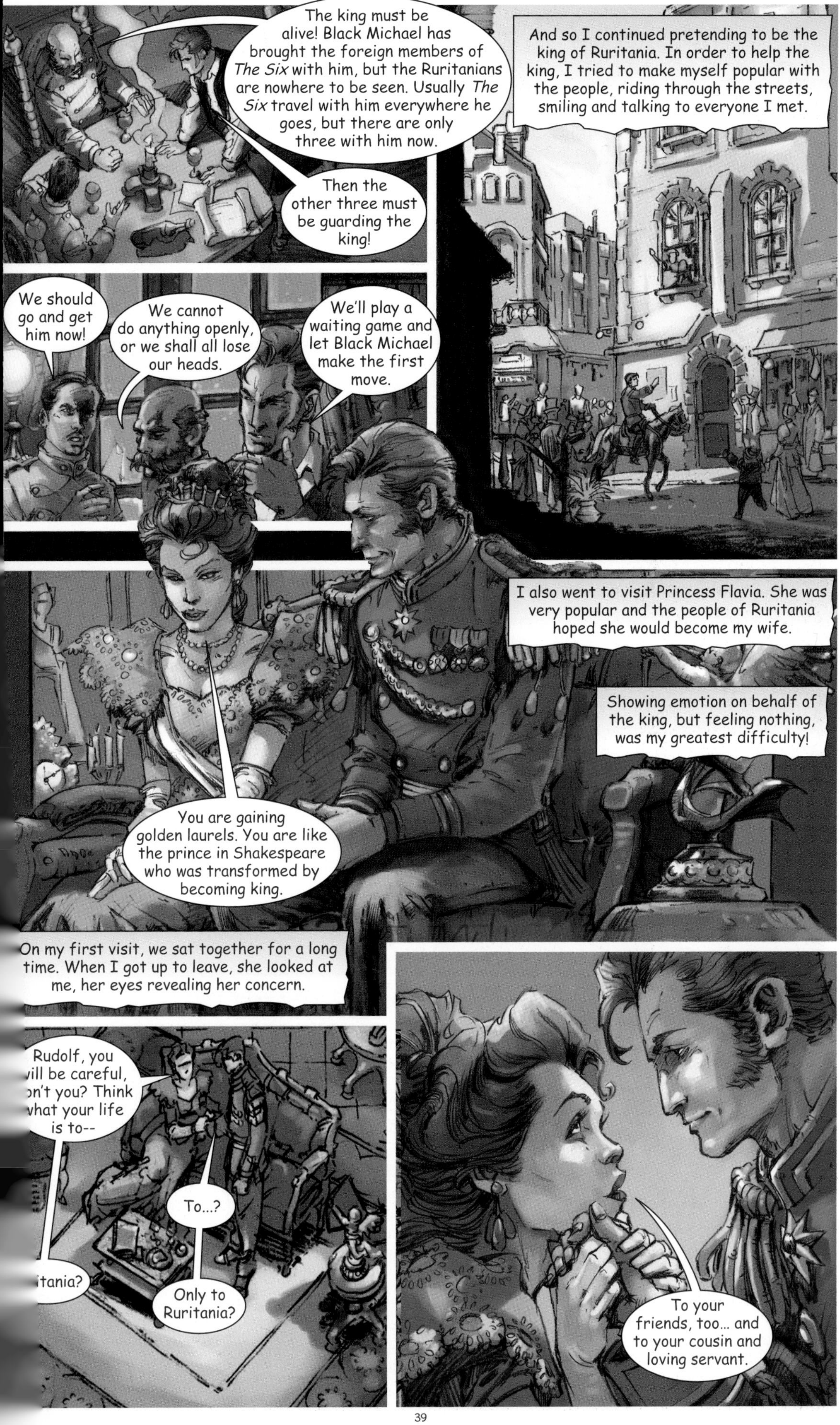

The king must be alive! Black Michael has brought the foreign members of *The Six* with him, but the Ruritanians are nowhere to be seen. Usually *The Six* travel with him everywhere he goes, but there are only three with him now.
Then the other three must be guarding the king!
And so I continued pretending to be the king of Ruritania. In order to help the king, I tried to make myself popular with the people, riding through the streets, smiling and talking to everyone I met.
We should go and get him now!
We cannot do anything openly, or we shall all lose our heads.
We'll play a waiting game and let Black Michael make the first move.
I also went to visit Princess Flavia. She was very popular and the people of Ruritania hoped she would become my wife.
Showing emotion on behalf of the king, but feeling nothing, was my greatest difficulty!
You are gaining golden laurels. You are like the prince in Shakespeare who was transformed by becoming king.
On my first visit, we sat together for a long time. When I got up to leave, she looked at me, her eyes revealing her concern.
Rudolf, you vill be careful, on't you? Think vhat your life is to--
To...?
itania?
Only to Ruritania?
To your friends, too... and to your cousin and loving servant.

One day, Sapt came into my room and threw a letter toward me.

That's for you— a woman's handwriting, I think. But I've got some news for you first.

The king is at the Castle of Zenda.

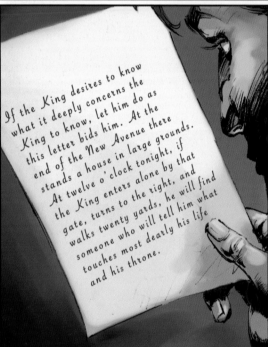

If the King desires to know what it deeply concerns the King to know, let him do as this letter bids him. At the end of the New Avenue there stands a house in large grounds. At twelve o'clock tonight, if the King enters alone by that gate, turns to the right, and walks twenty yards, he will find someone who will tell him what touches most dearly his life and his throne.

If you hesitate, consult Colonel Sapt. Ask him what woman would do most to prevent the duke from marrying his cousin, and therefore, most to prevent him becoming king? And ask if her name begins with — A?

Antoinette de Mauban, by heavens! She wants to marry the Duke, Black Michael.

That's true. But you must not go. They'll kill you. I believe that Michael wrote this letter.

Every day we are playing against time and the king's life is in danger. Every day that I masquerade like this, there is fresh risk. Sapt, we must play high...

...we must force the game.

So be it. If you're going, I'll come with you.

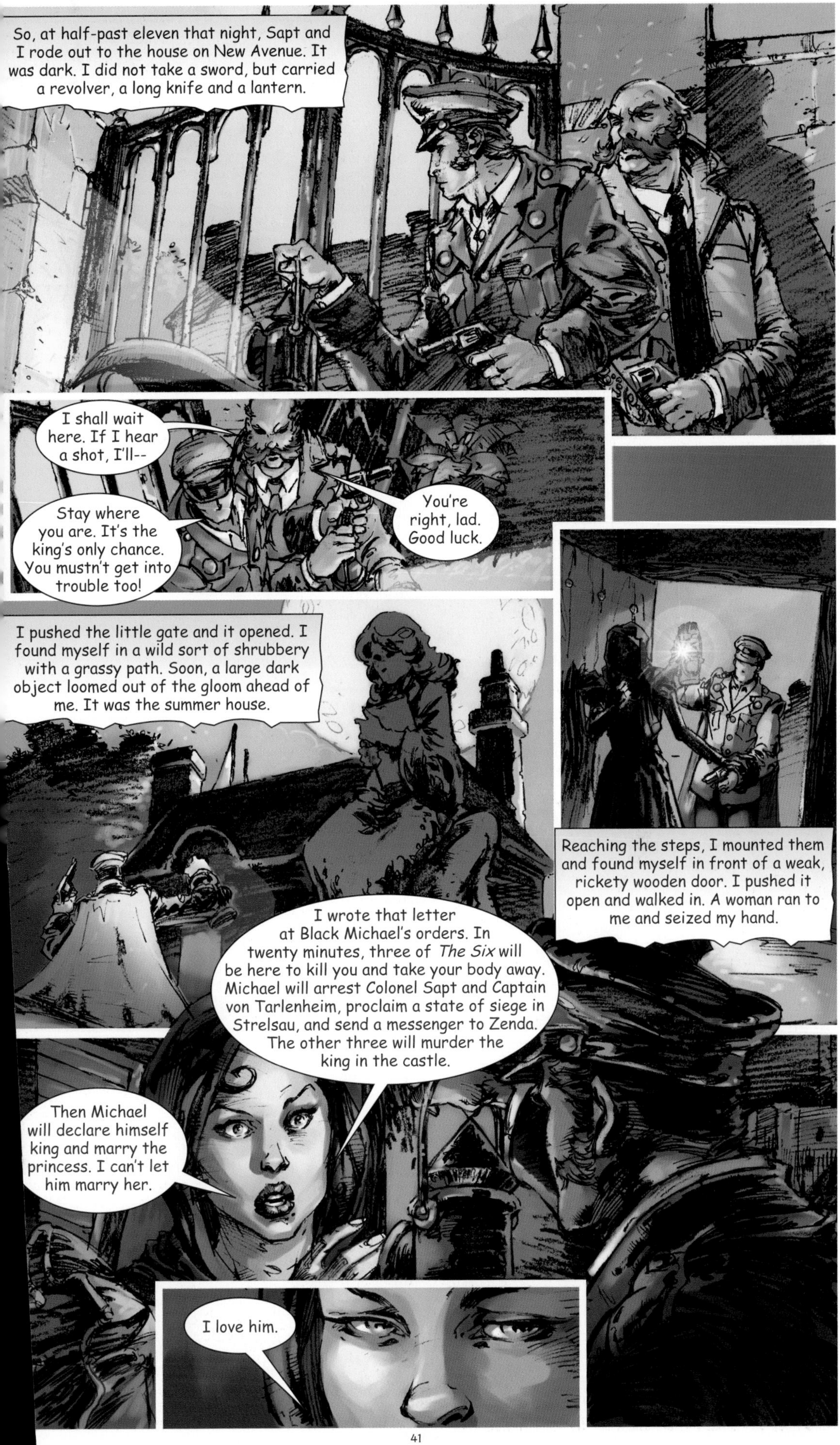

So, at half-past eleven that night, Sapt and I rode out to the house on New Avenue. It was dark. I did not take a sword, but carried a revolver, a long knife and a lantern.
I shall wait here. If I hear a shot, I'll--
Stay where you are. It's the king's only chance. You mustn't get into trouble too!
You're right, lad. Good luck.
I pushed the little gate and it opened. I found myself in a wild sort of shrubbery with a grassy path. Soon, a large dark object loomed out of the gloom ahead of me. It was the summer house.
Reaching the steps, I mounted them and found myself in front of a weak, rickety wooden door. I pushed it open and walked in. A woman ran to me and seized my hand.
I wrote that letter at Black Michael's orders. In twenty minutes, three of *The Six* will be here to kill you and take your body away. Michael will arrest Colonel Sapt and Captain von Tarlenheim, proclaim a state of siege in Strelsau, and send a messenger to Zenda. The other three will murder the king in the castle.
Then Michael will declare himself king and marry the princess. I can't let him marry her.
I love him.

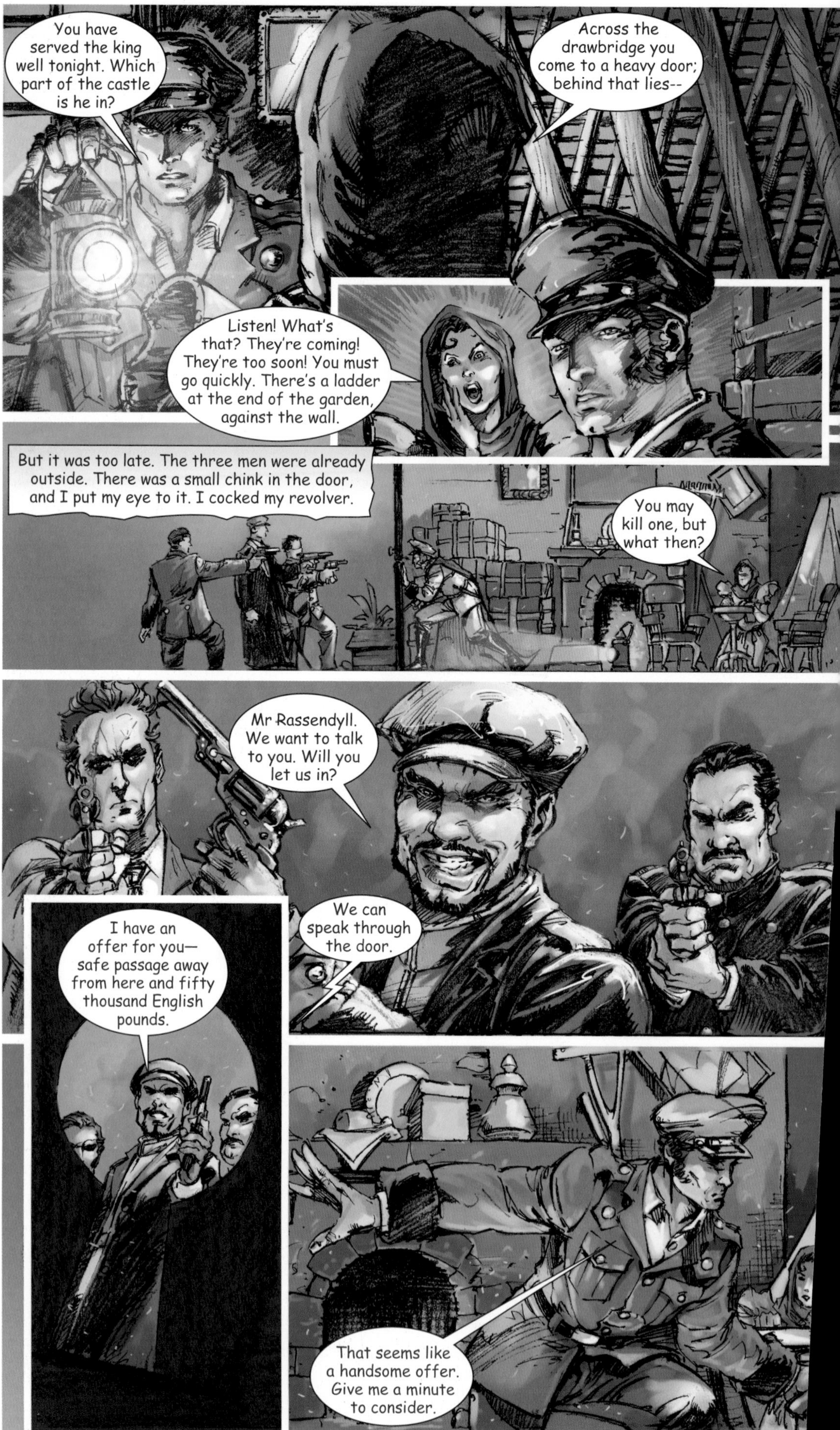

You have served the king well tonight. Which part of the castle is he in?
Across the drawbridge you come to a heavy door; behind that lies--
Listen! What's that? They're coming! They're too soon! You must go quickly. There's a ladder at the end of the garden, against the wall.
But it was too late. The three men were already outside. There was a small chink in the door, and I put my eye to it. I cocked my revolver.
You may kill one, but what then?
Mr Rassendyll. We want to talk to you. Will you let us in?
We can speak through the door.
I have an offer for you— safe passage away from here and fifty thousand English pounds.
That seems like a handsome offer. Give me a minute to consider.

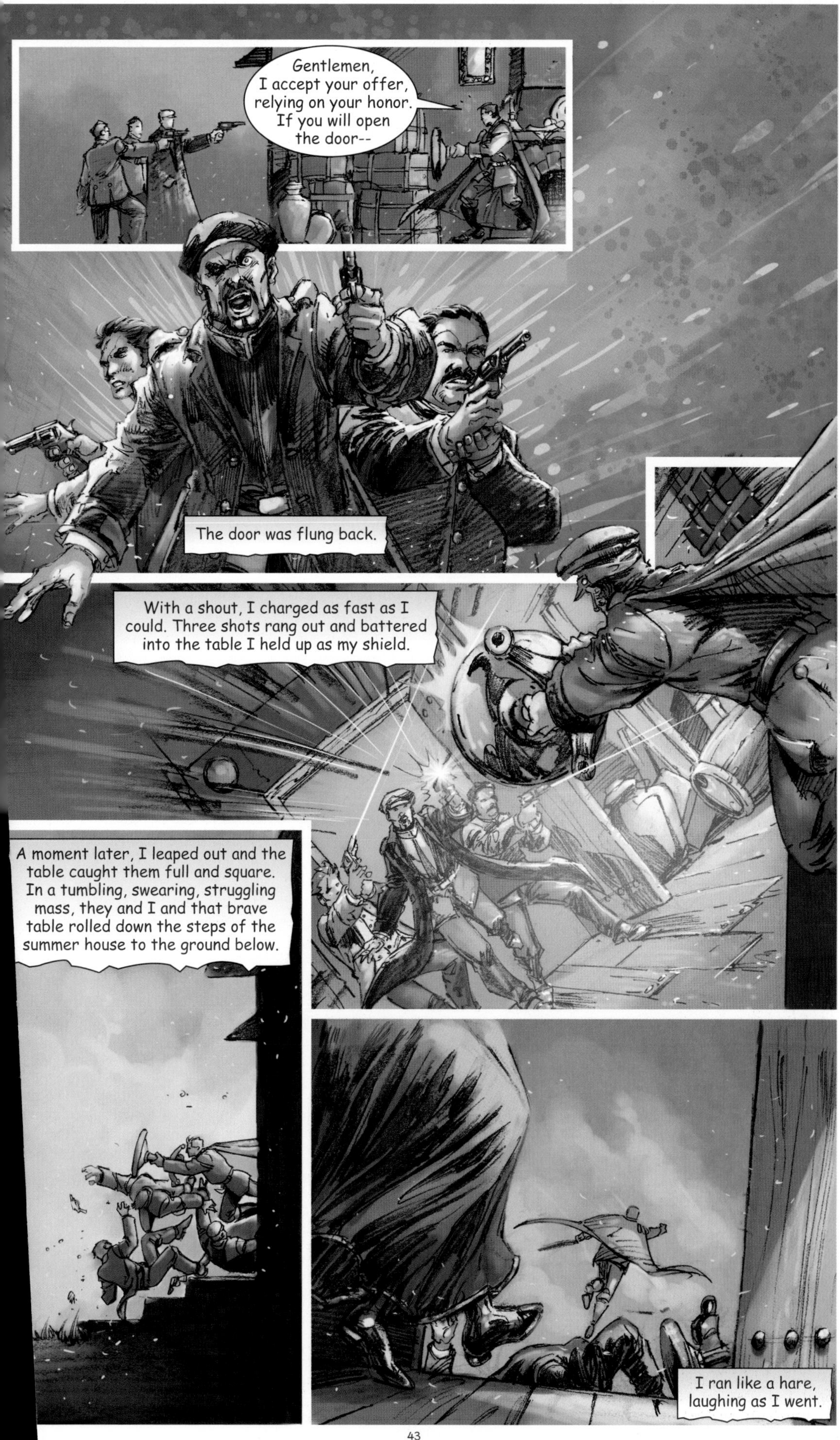
Gentlemen, I accept your offer, relying on your honor. If you will open the door--
The door was flung back.
With a shout, I charged as fast as I could. Three shots rang out and battered into the table I held up as my shield.
A moment later, I leaped out and the table caught them full and square. In a tumbling, swearing, struggling mass, they and I and that brave table rolled down the steps of the summer house to the ground below.
I ran like a hare, laughing as I went.

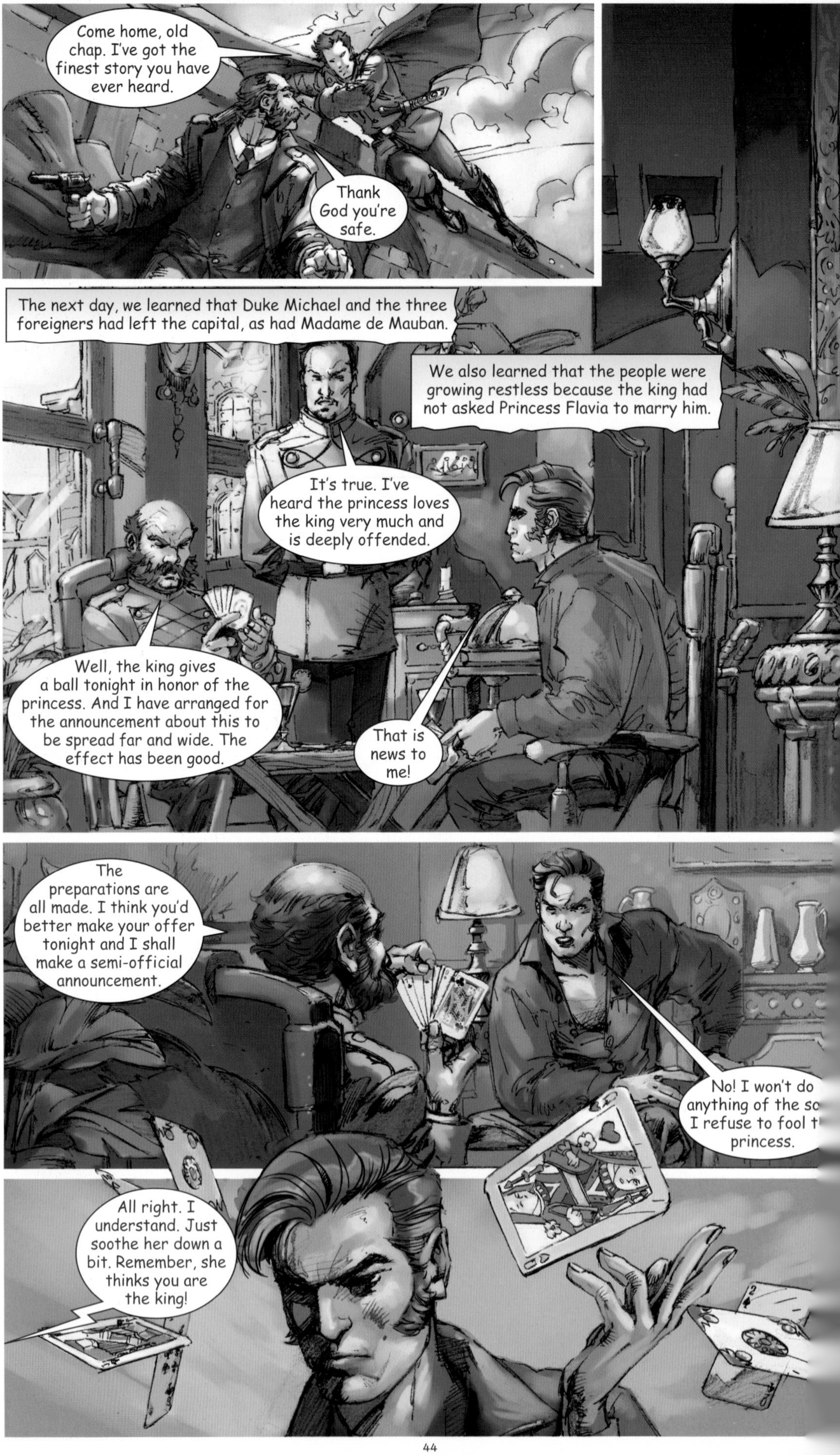
Come home, old chap. I've got the finest story you have ever heard.
Thank God you're safe.
The next day, we learned that Duke Michael and the three foreigners had left the capital, as had Madame de Mauban.
We also learned that the people were growing restless because the king had not asked Princess Flavia to marry him.
It's true. I've heard the princess loves the king very much and is deeply offended.
Well, the king gives a ball tonight in honor of the princess. And I have arranged for the announcement about this to be spread far and wide. The effect has been good.
That is news to me!
The preparations are all made. I think you'd better make your offer tonight and I shall make a semi-official announcement.
No! I won't do anything of the so
I refuse to fool t
princess.
All right. I understand. Just soothe her down a bit. Remember, she thinks you are the king!

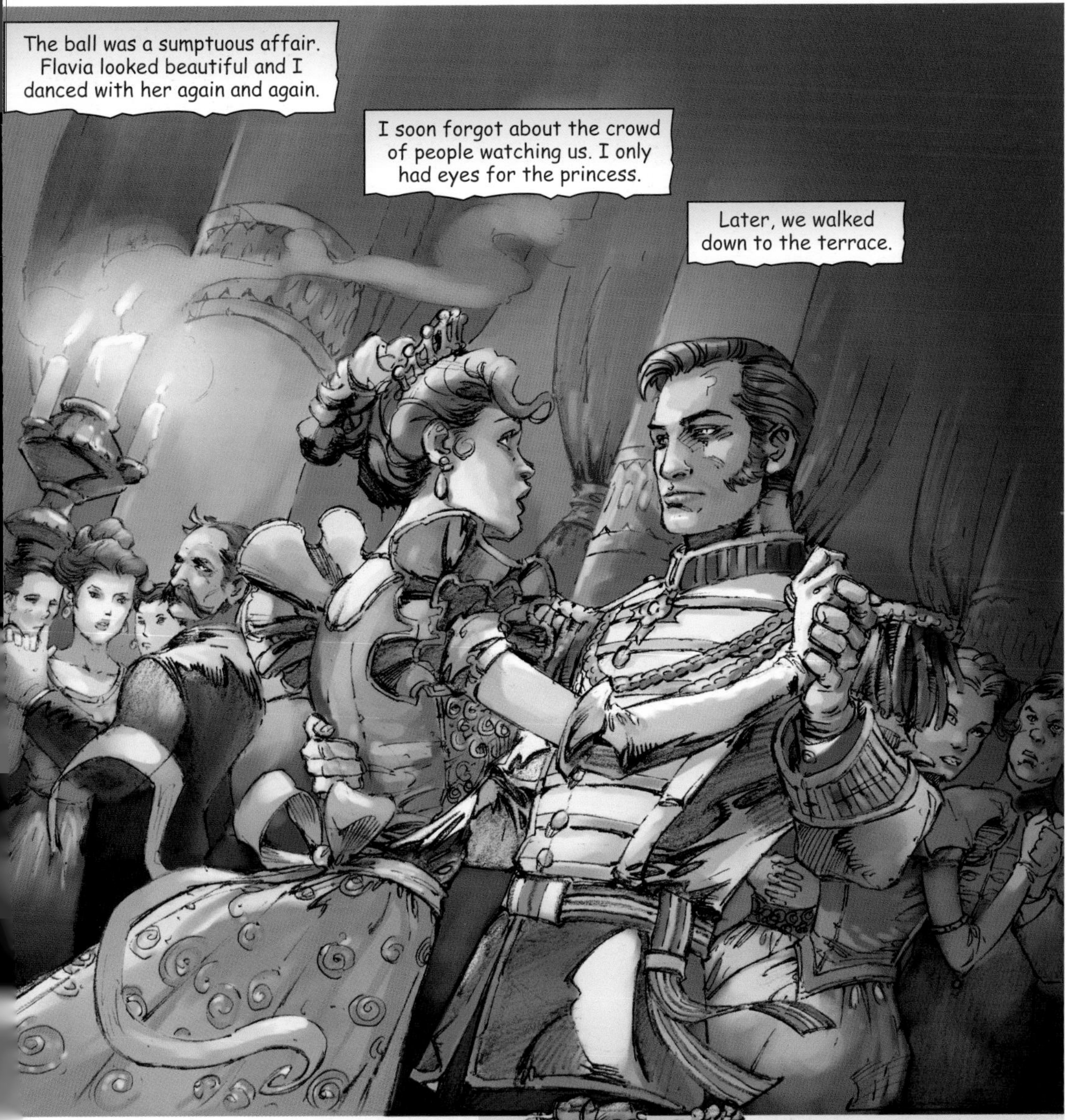
The ball was a sumptuous affair. Flavia looked beautiful and I danced with her again and again.
I soon forgot about the crowd of people watching us. I only had eyes for the princess.
Later, we walked down to the terrace.

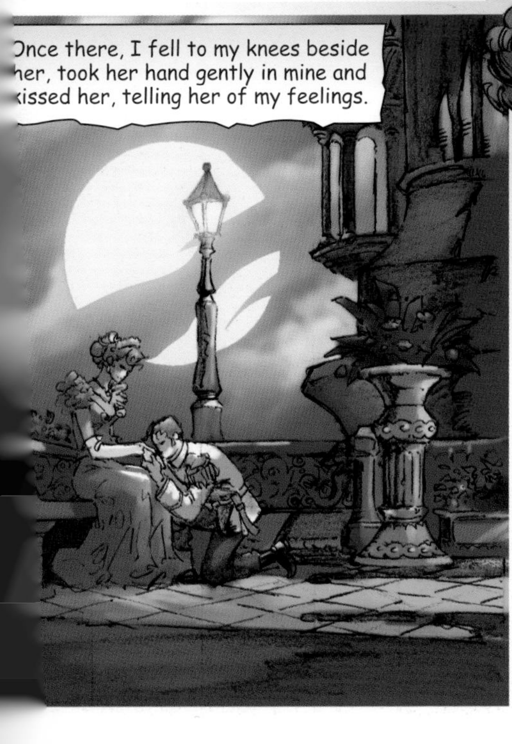
Once there, I fell to my knees beside her, took her hand gently in mine and kissed her, telling her of my feelings.

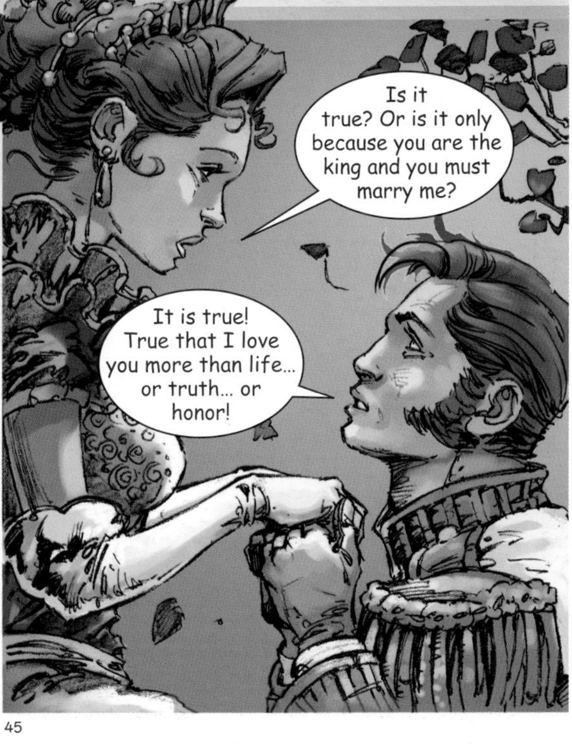
Is it true? Or is it only because you are the king and you must marry me?
It is true! True that I love you more than life... or truth... or honor!

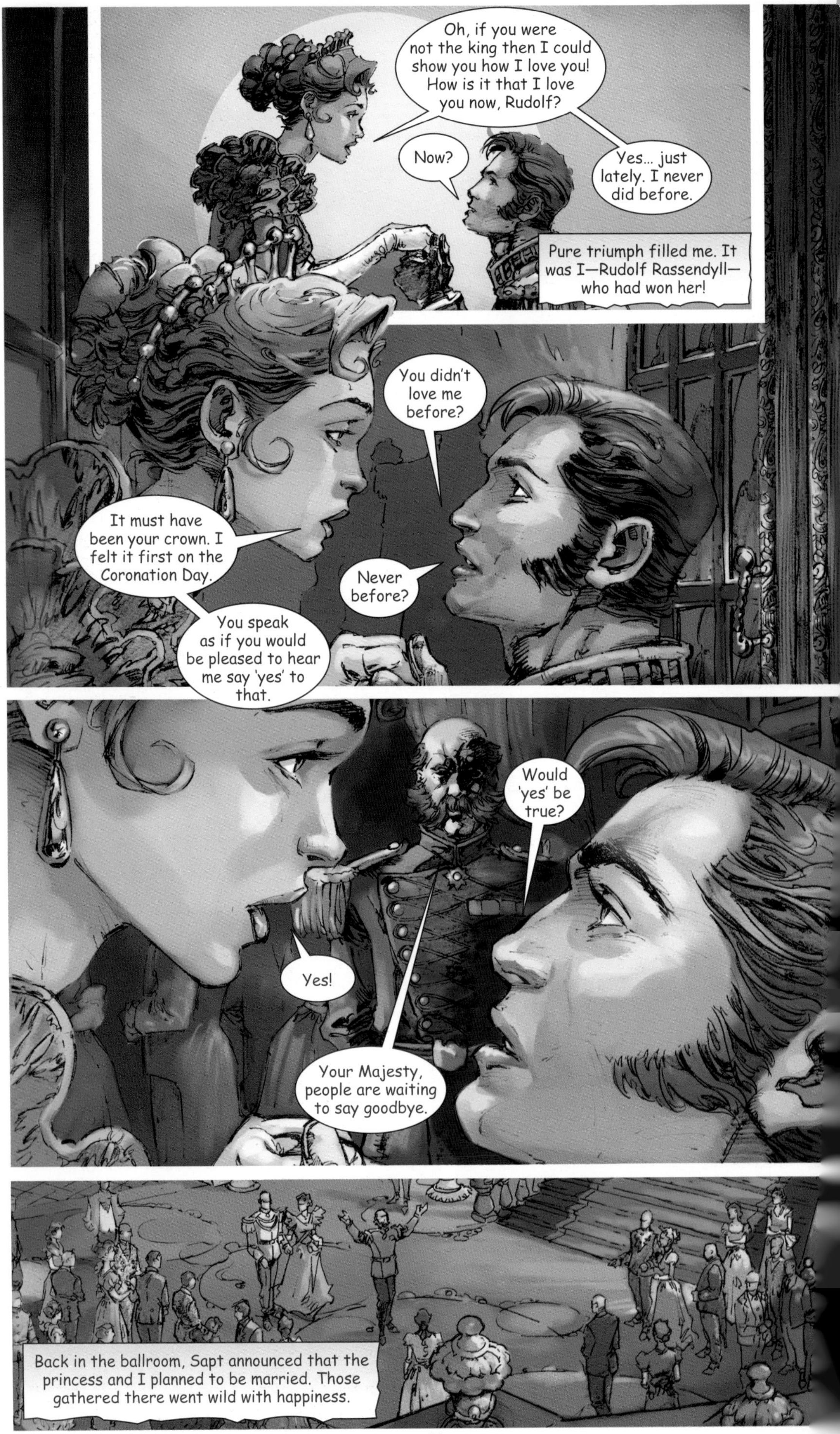
Oh, if you were not the king then I could show you how I love you! How is it that I love you now, Rudolf?
Now?
Yes... just lately. I never did before.
Pure triumph filled me. It was I—Rudolf Rassendyll—who had won her!
You didn't love me before?
It must have been your crown. I felt it first on the Coronation Day.
Never before?
You speak as if you would be pleased to hear me say 'yes' to that.
Would 'yes' be true?
Yes!
Your Majesty, people are waiting to say goodbye.
Back in the ballroom, Sapt announced that the princess and I planned to be married. Those gathered there went wild with happiness.

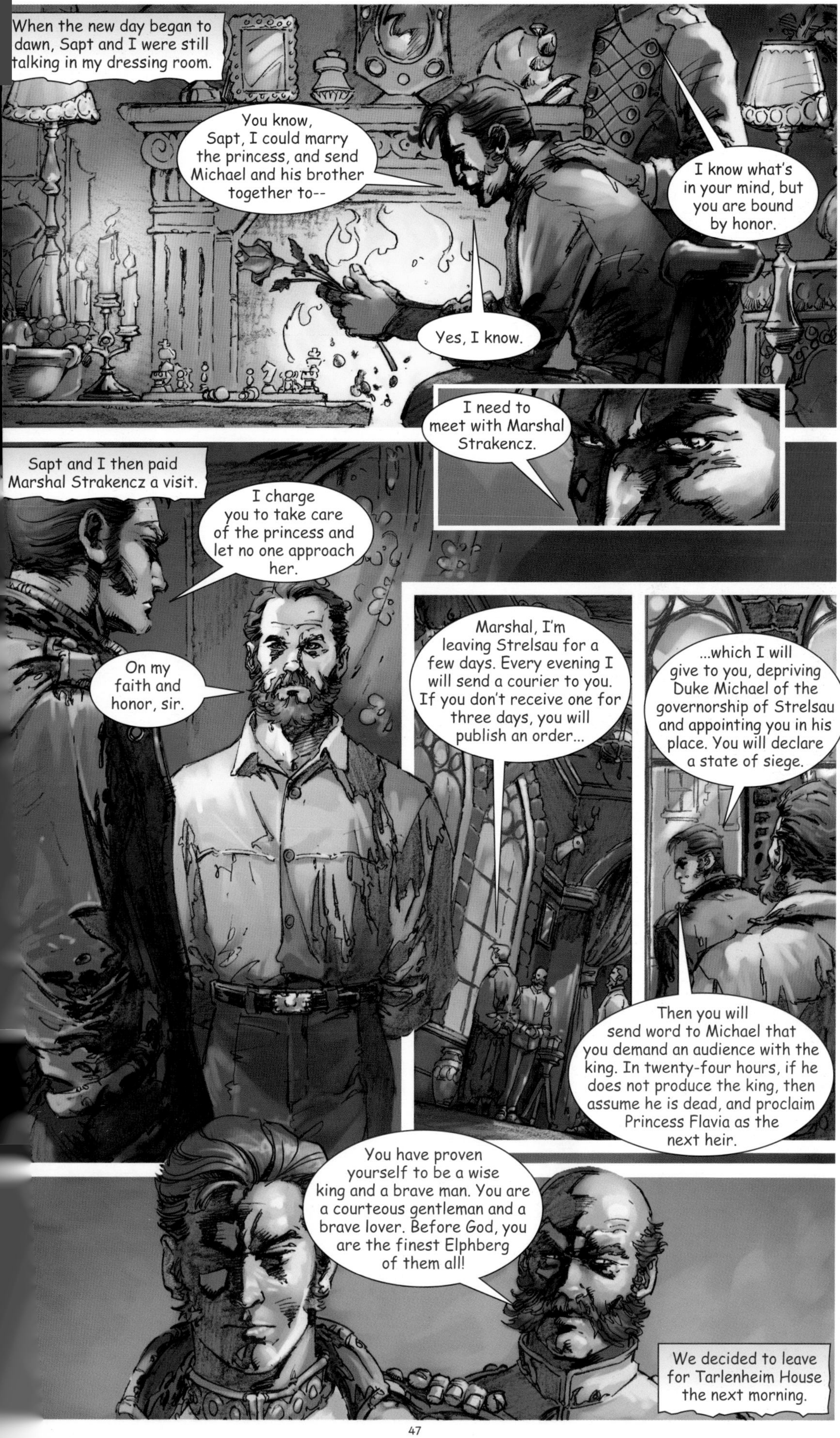
When the new day began to dawn, Sapt and I were still talking in my dressing room.
You know, Sapt, I could marry the princess, and send Michael and his brother together to--
I know what's in your mind, but you are bound by honor.
Yes, I know.
I need to meet with Marshal Strakencz.
Sapt and I then paid Marshal Strakencz a visit.
I charge you to take care of the princess and let no one approach her.
On my faith and honor, sir.
Marshal, I'm leaving Strelsau for a few days. Every evening I will send a courier to you. If you don't receive one for three days, you will publish an order...
...which I will give to you, depriving Duke Michael of the governorship of Strelsau and appointing you in his place. You will declare a state of siege.
Then you will send word to Michael that you demand an audience with the king. In twenty-four hours, if he does not produce the king, then assume he is dead, and proclaim Princess Flavia as the next heir.
You have proven yourself to be a wise king and a brave man. You are a courteous gentleman and a brave lover. Before God, you are the finest Elphberg of them all!
We decided to leave for Tarlenheim House the next morning.

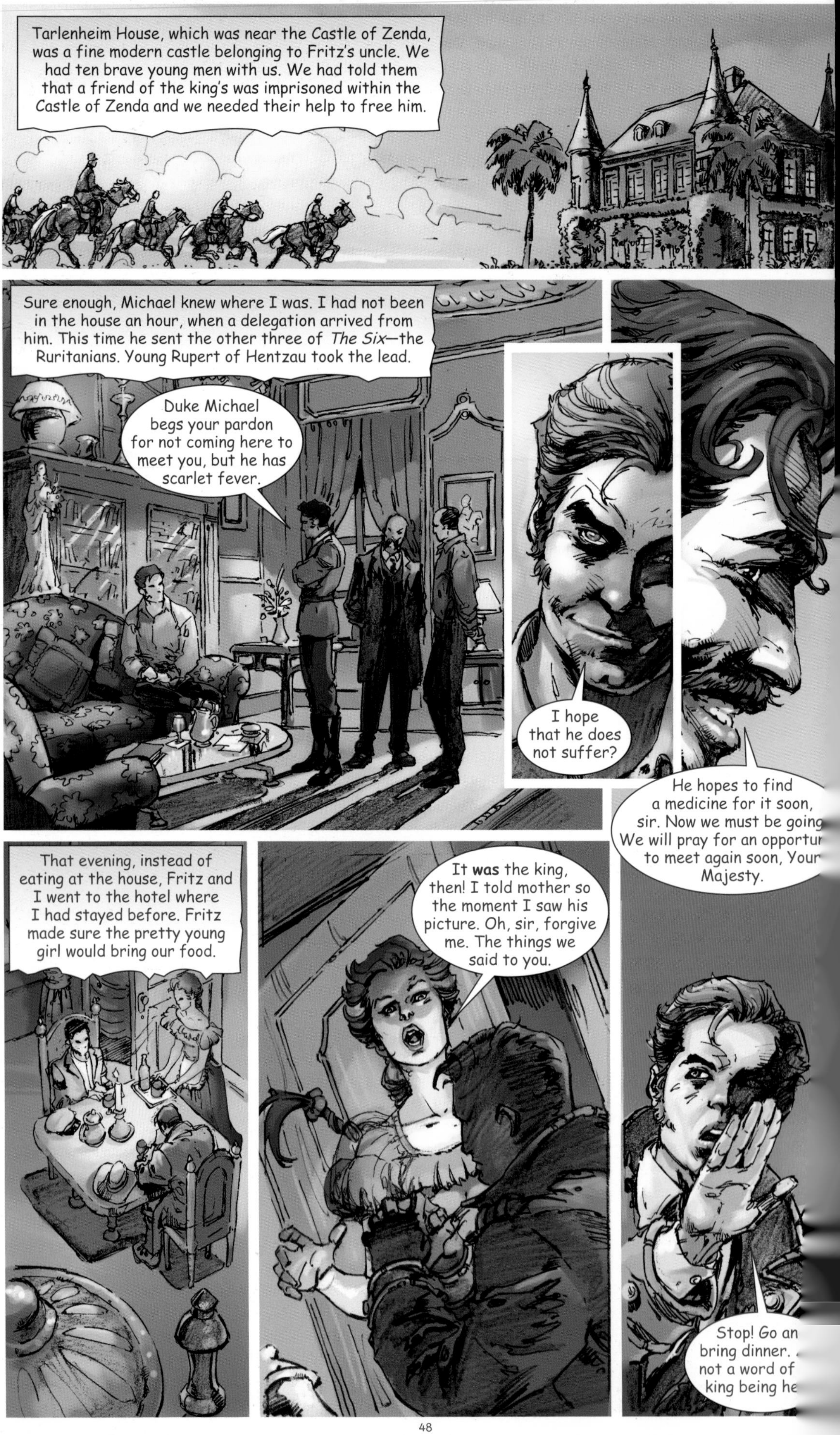
Tarlenheim House, which was near the Castle of Zenda, was a fine modern castle belonging to Fritz's uncle. We had ten brave young men with us. We had told them that a friend of the king's was imprisoned within the Castle of Zenda and we needed their help to free him.
Sure enough, Michael knew where I was. I had not been in the house an hour, when a delegation arrived from him. This time he sent the other three of *The Six*—the Ruritanians. Young Rupert of Hentzau took the lead.
Duke Michael begs your pardon for not coming here to meet you, but he has scarlet fever.
I hope that he does not suffer?
He hopes to find a medicine for it soon, sir. Now we must be going We will pray for an opportur to meet again soon, Your Majesty.
That evening, instead of eating at the house, Fritz and I went to the hotel where I had stayed before. Fritz made sure the pretty young girl would bring our food.
It **was** the king, then! I told mother so the moment I saw his picture. Oh, sir, forgive me. The things we said to you.
Stop! Go an bring dinner. not a word of king being he

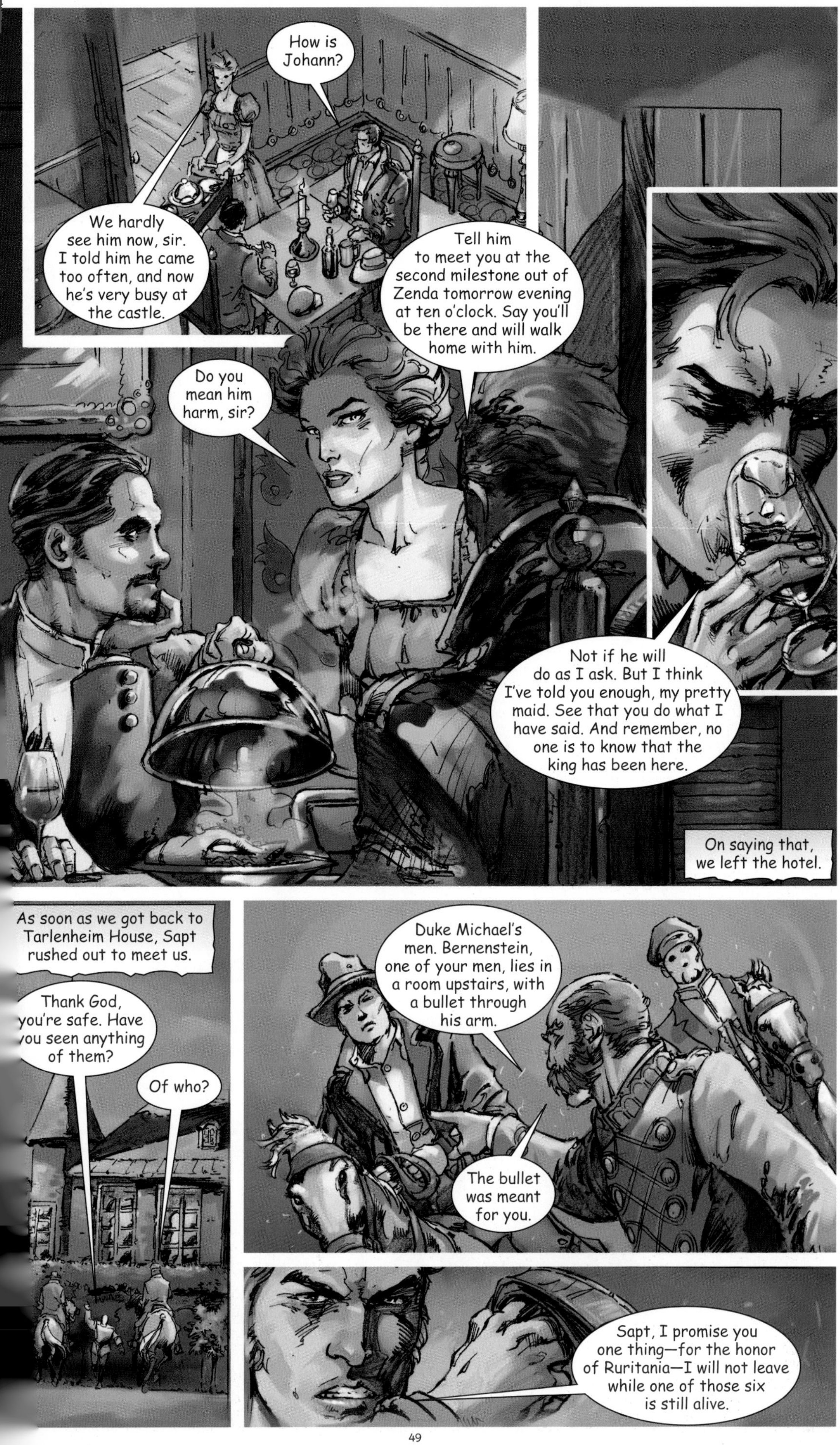
How is Johann?
We hardly see him now, sir. I told him he came too often, and now he's very busy at the castle.
Tell him to meet you at the second milestone out of Zenda tomorrow evening at ten o'clock. Say you'll be there and will walk home with him.
Do you mean him harm, sir?
Not if he will do as I ask. But I think I've told you enough, my pretty maid. See that you do what I have said. And remember, no one is to know that the king has been here.
On saying that, we left the hotel.
As soon as we got back to Tarlenheim House, Sapt rushed out to meet us.
Thank God, you're safe. Have you seen anything of them?
Of who?
Duke Michael's men. Bernenstein, one of your men, lies in a room upstairs, with a bullet through his arm.
The bullet was meant for you.
Sapt, I promise you one thing—for the honor of Ruritania—I will not leave while one of those six is still alive.

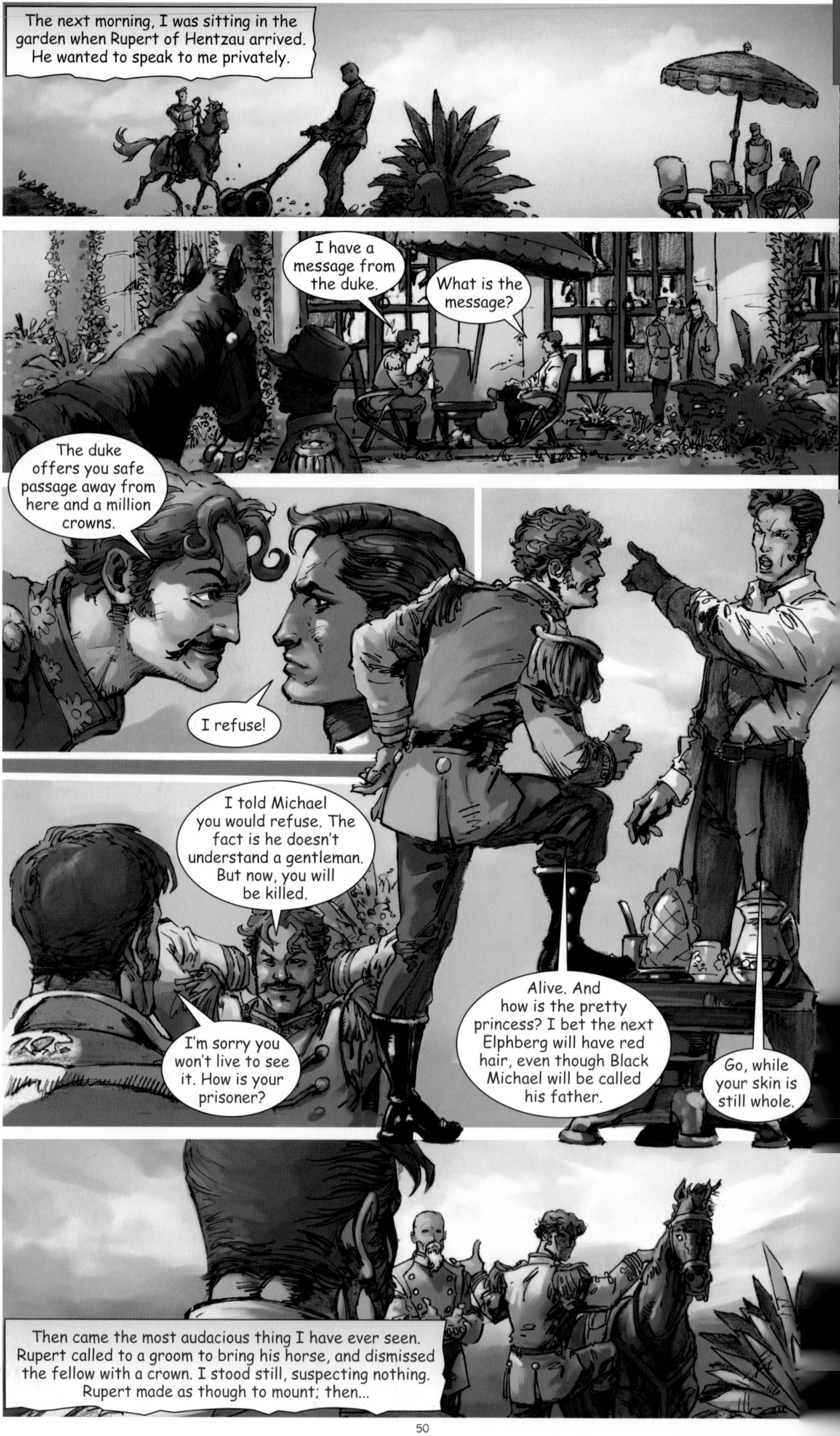
The next morning, I was sitting in the garden when Rupert of Hentzau arrived. He wanted to speak to me privately.
I have a message from the duke.
What is the message?
The duke offers you safe passage away from here and a million crowns.
I refuse!
I told Michael you would refuse. The fact is he doesn't understand a gentleman. But now, you will be killed.
I'm sorry you won't live to see it. How is your prisoner?
Alive. And how is the pretty princess? I bet the next Elphberg will have red hair, even though Black Michael will be called his father.
Go, while your skin is still whole.
Then came the most audacious thing I have ever seen. Rupert called to a groom to bring his horse, and dismissed the fellow with a crown. I stood still, suspecting nothing. Rupert made as though to mount; then...

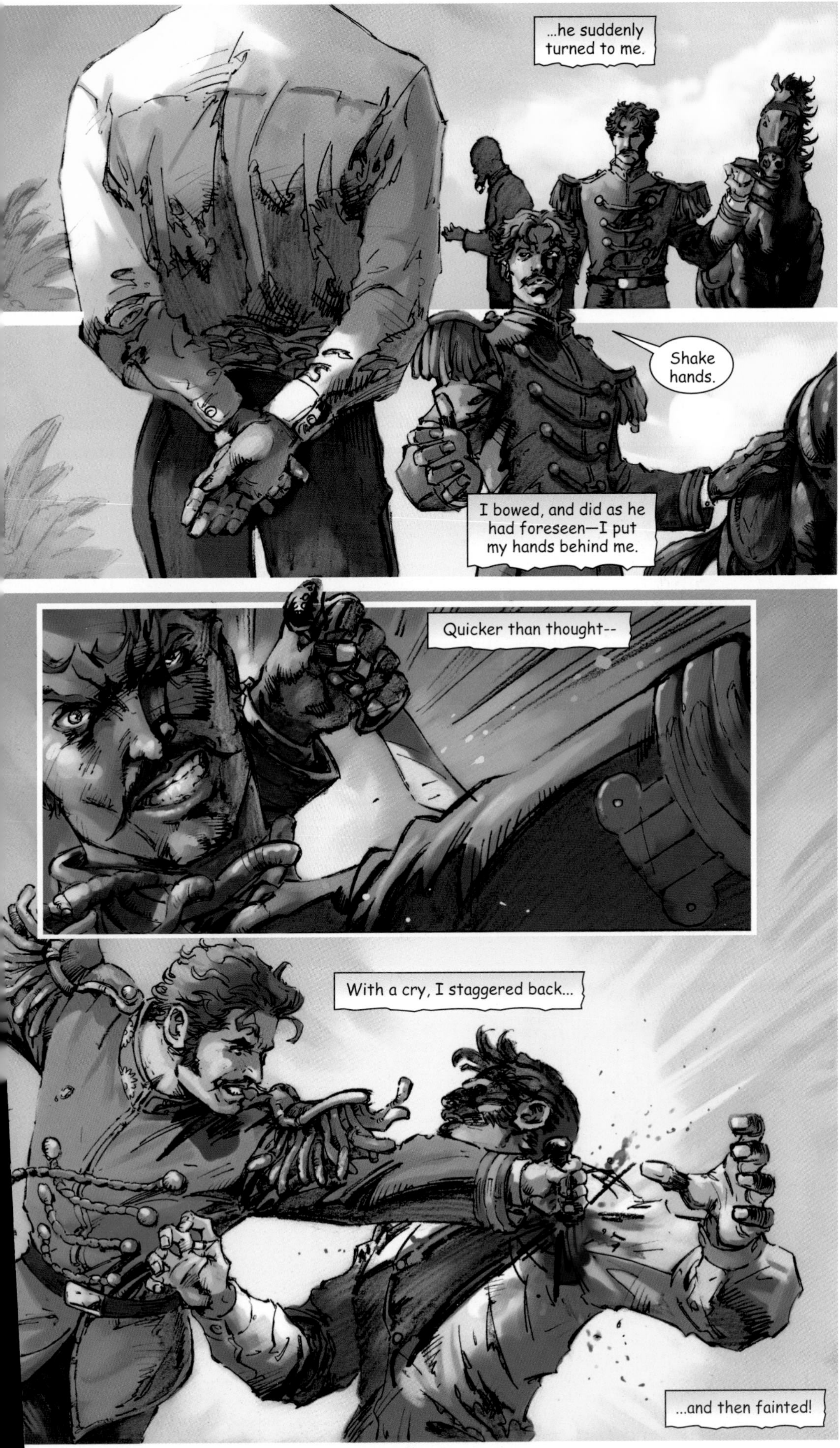
...he suddenly turned to me.
Shake hands.
I bowed, and did as he had foreseen—I put my hands behind me.
Quicker than thought--
With a cry, I staggered back...
...and then fainted!

When I awoke, it was dark.

You were not badly hurt and your wound will soon heal.

The plan to catch young Johann has worked. He seems pleased to be here. I think he is afraid of the duke.

Later, Sapt brought Johann to see me. At first, he was afraid to speak, but then he began to talk. We asked him many questions and, finally, he gave us the information we wanted.

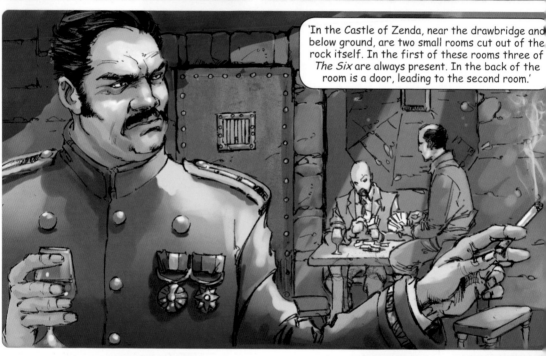

'In the Castle of Zenda, near the drawbridge and below ground, are two small rooms cut out of the rock itself. In the first of these rooms three of *The Six* are always present. In the back of the room is a door, leading to the second room.'

'The king is in the second room.'

If someone tries to enter the first room, two of the men will fight them, and the third will run into the second room and kill the king.

'There's a window in the second room opens into a large pipe that drops i the moat. They will tie a stone to t king's body and drop it down the pi

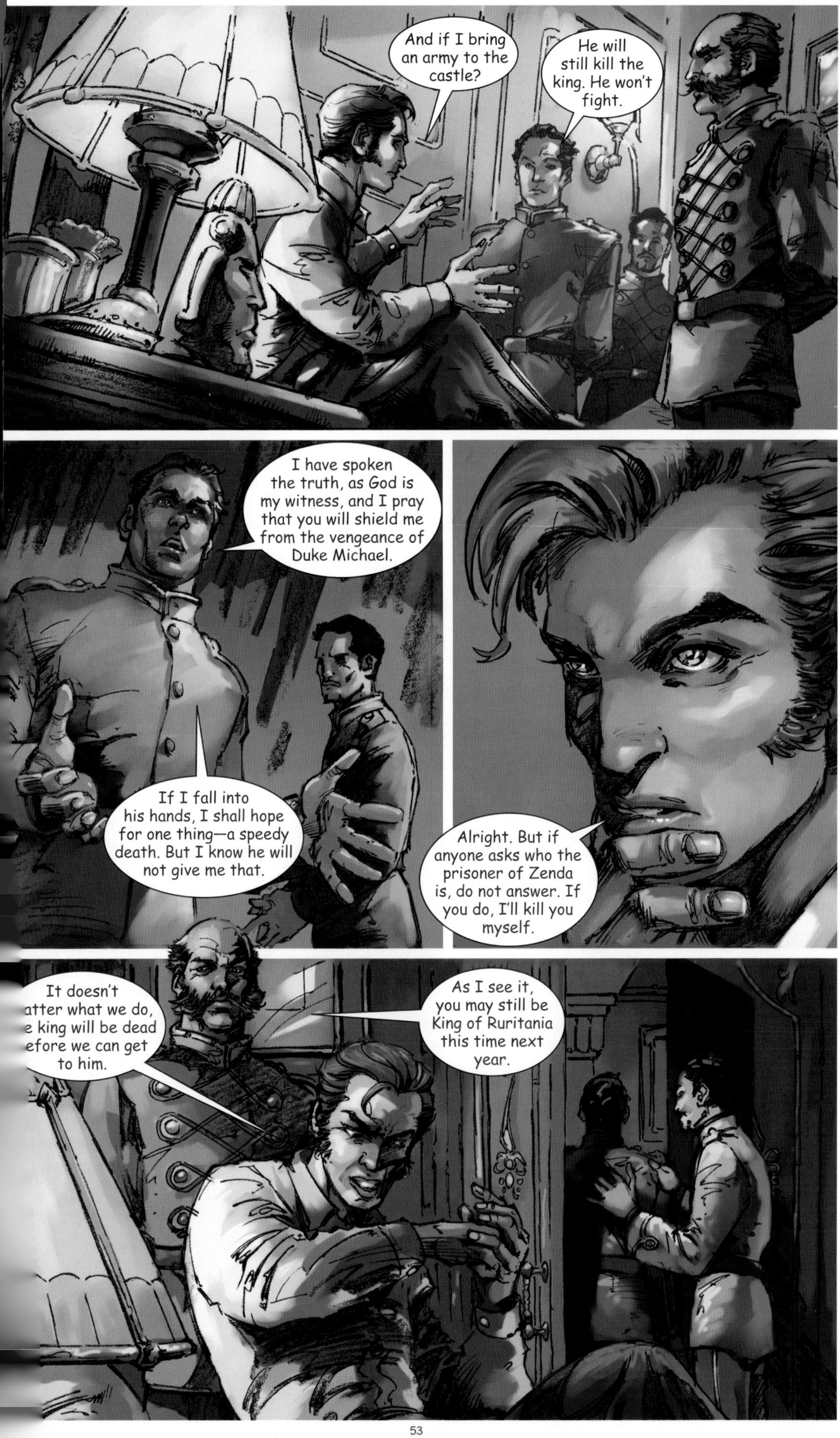
And if I bring an army to the castle?
He will still kill the king. He won't fight.
I have spoken the truth, as God is my witness, and I pray that you will shield me from the vengeance of Duke Michael.
If I fall into his hands, I shall hope for one thing—a speedy death. But I know he will not give me that.
Alright. But if anyone asks who the prisoner of Zenda is, do not answer. If you do, I'll kill you myself.
It doesn't atter what we do, e king will be dead efore we can get to him.
As I see it, you may still be King of Ruritania this time next year.

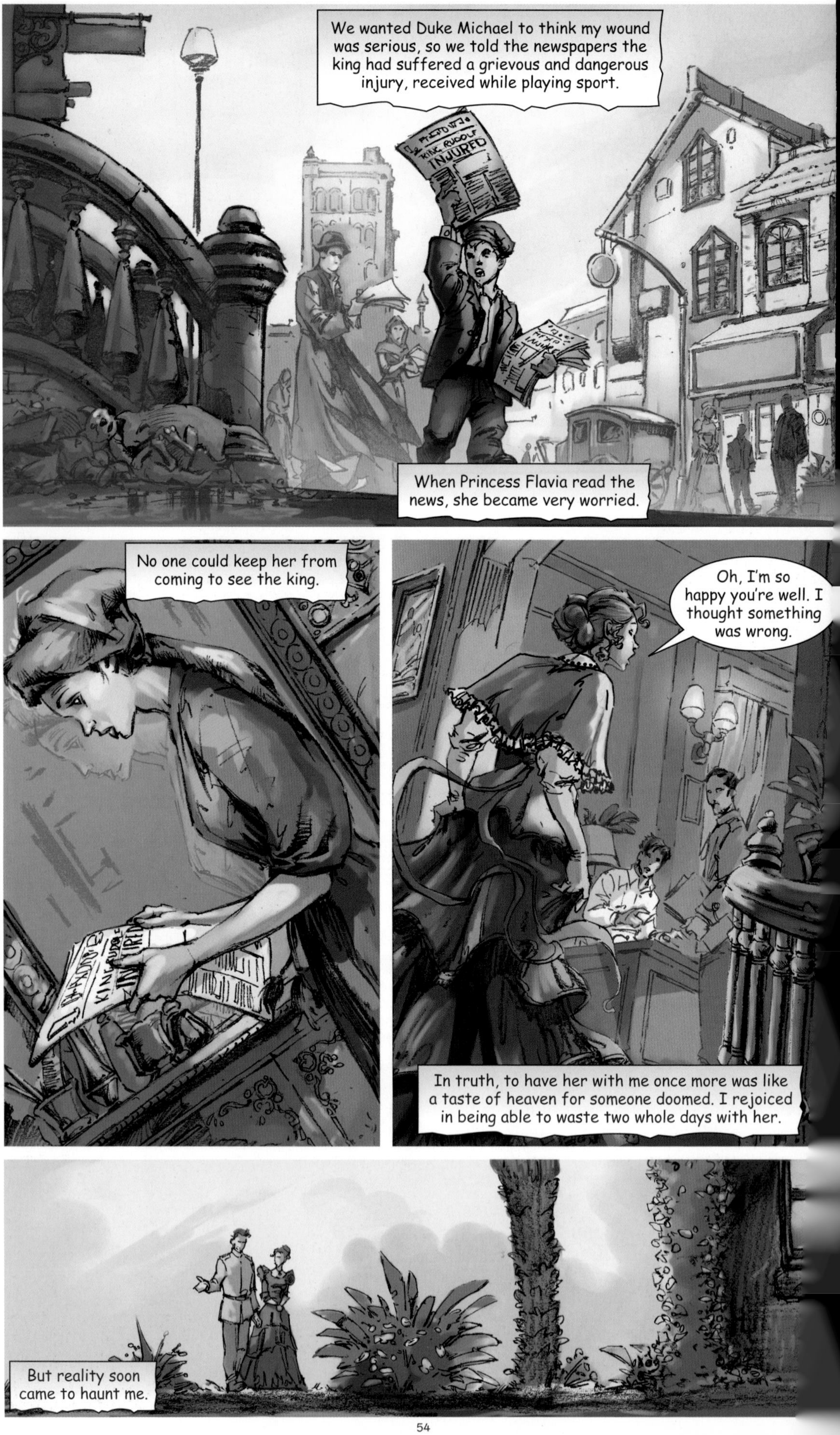
We wanted Duke Michael to think my wound was serious, so we told the newspapers the king had suffered a grievous and dangerous injury, received while playing sport.
KING RUDOLF
INJURED
When Princess Flavia read the news, she became very worried.
No one could keep her from coming to see the king.
Oh, I'm so happy you're well. I thought something was wrong.
In truth, to have her with me once more was like a taste of heaven for someone doomed. I rejoiced in being able to waste two whole days with her.
But reality soon came to haunt me.

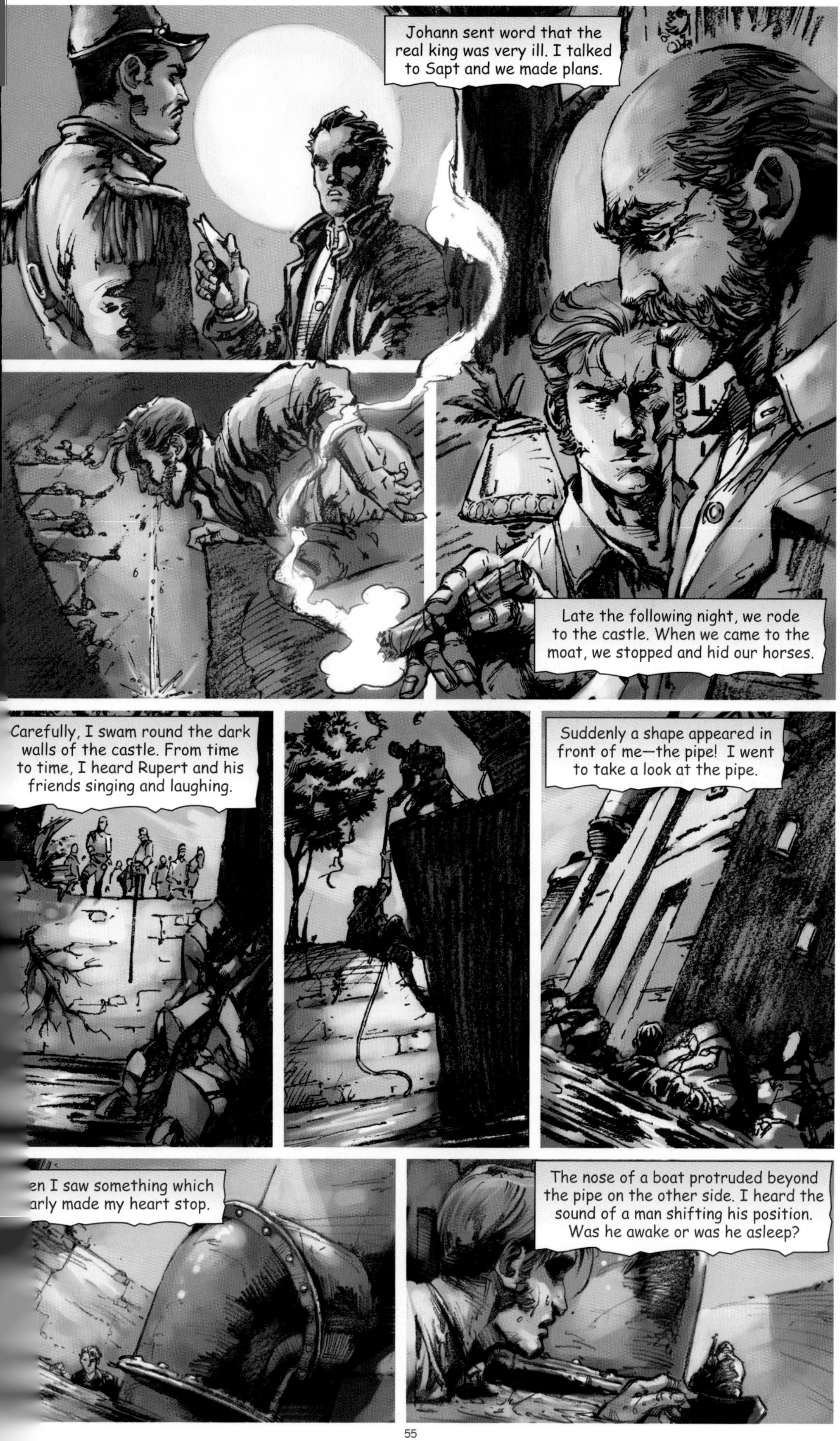

Johann sent word that the real king was very ill. I talked to Sapt and we made plans.
Late the following night, we rode to the castle. When we came to the moat, we stopped and hid our horses.
Carefully, I swam round the dark walls of the castle. From time to time, I heard Rupert and his friends singing and laughing.
Suddenly a shape appeared in front of me—the pipe! I went to take a look at the pipe.
en I saw something which arly made my heart stop.
The nose of a boat protruded beyond the pipe on the other side. I heard the sound of a man shifting his position. Was he awake or was he asleep?

Fortunately, the watchman in the boat was sleeping. I had to do something before he woke up and discovered me.

As I struck home with my knife, I heard the chorus of a love song from the opposite bank.

Looking through a gap at the bottom of the pipe, I could see the king... and Detchard, the Englishman.

Just then, someone shouted—calling out to the watchman I had just killed.

My task now was to get myself away in safety. Ge[t] into the boat, I rowed swiftly round to where [my] friends were waiting. I had just reached the sp[ot] when a loud whistle sounded over the moat behin[d]

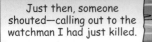

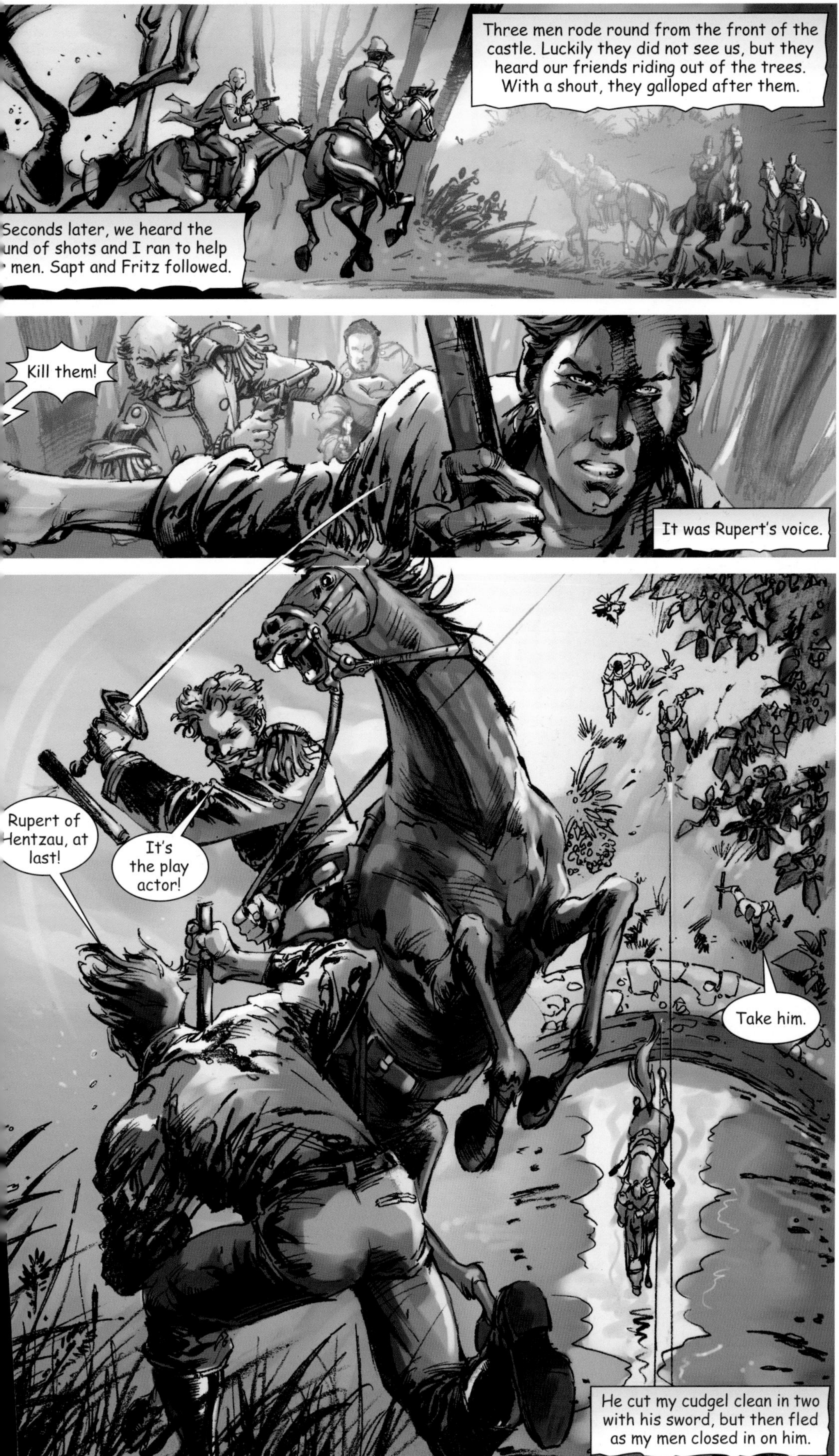
Three men rode round from the front of the castle. Luckily they did not see us, but they heard our friends riding out of the trees. With a shout, they galloped after them.
Seconds later, we heard the
und of shots and I ran to help
men. Sapt and Fritz followed.
Kill them!
It was Rupert's voice.
Rupert of Hentzau, at last!
It's the play actor!
Take him.
He cut my cudgel clean in two with his sword, but then fled as my men closed in on him.

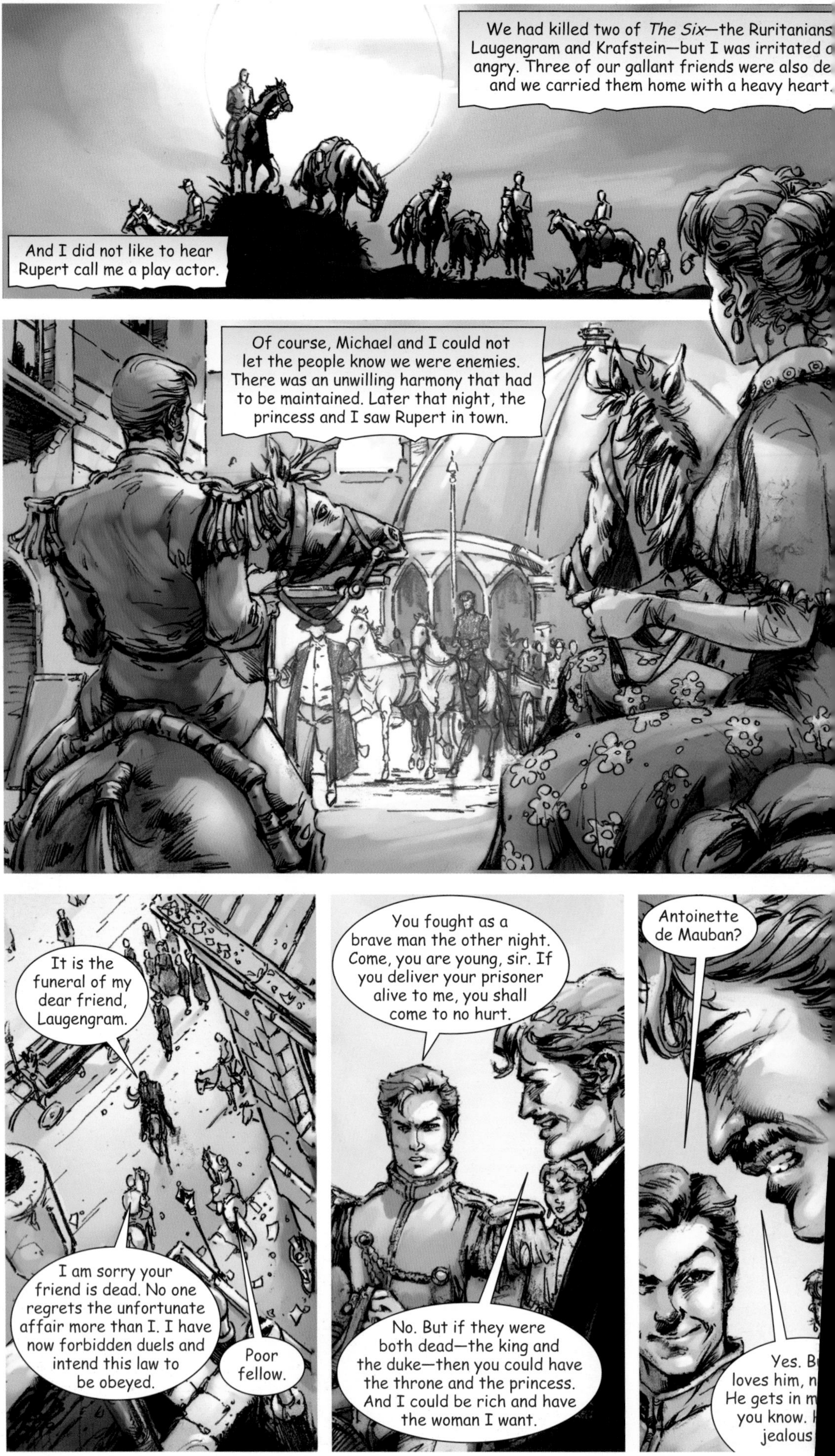

We had killed two of *The Six*—the Ruritanians Laugengram and Krafstein—but I was irritated a angry. Three of our gallant friends were also de and we carried them home with a heavy heart.
And I did not like to hear Rupert call me a play actor.
Of course, Michael and I could not let the people know we were enemies. There was an unwilling harmony that had to be maintained. Later that night, the princess and I saw Rupert in town.
It is the funeral of my dear friend, Laugengram.
I am sorry your friend is dead. No one regrets the unfortunate affair more than I. I have now forbidden duels and intend this law to be obeyed.
Poor fellow.
You fought as a brave man the other night. Come, you are young, sir. If you deliver your prisoner alive to me, you shall come to no hurt.
No. But if they were both dead—the king and the duke—then you could have the throne and the princess. And I could be rich and have the woman I want.
Antoinette de Mauban?
Yes. B loves him, n He gets in m you know. jealous

Princess Flavia thought young Rupert very handsome, but that he looked sad at his friend's death.

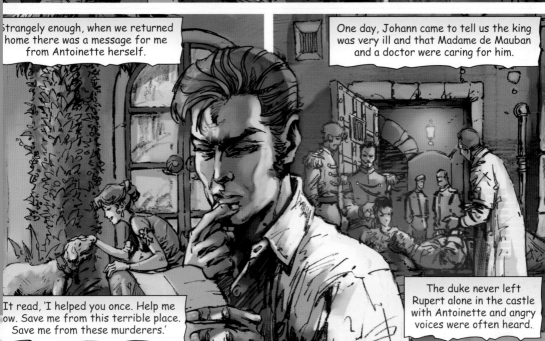

Strangely enough, when we returned home there was a message for me from Antoinette herself.

One day, Johann came to tell us the king was very ill and that Madame de Mauban and a doctor were caring for him.

It read, 'I helped you once. Help me now. Save me from this terrible place. Save me from these murderers.'

The duke never left Rupert alone in the castle with Antoinette and angry voices were often heard.

Johann, you shall have fifty thousand crowns if you do what I ask of you tomorrow night.

Carry this note to Madame de Mauban and, at exactly two in the morning, open the front door of the castle—and then escape as quickly as your legs will carry you.

Johann was trembling, but I had to trust him, for I feared the king would die.

I explained my plan to my loyal friends, Sapt and Fritz. It was a dangerous and complicated plan—but we had to try!

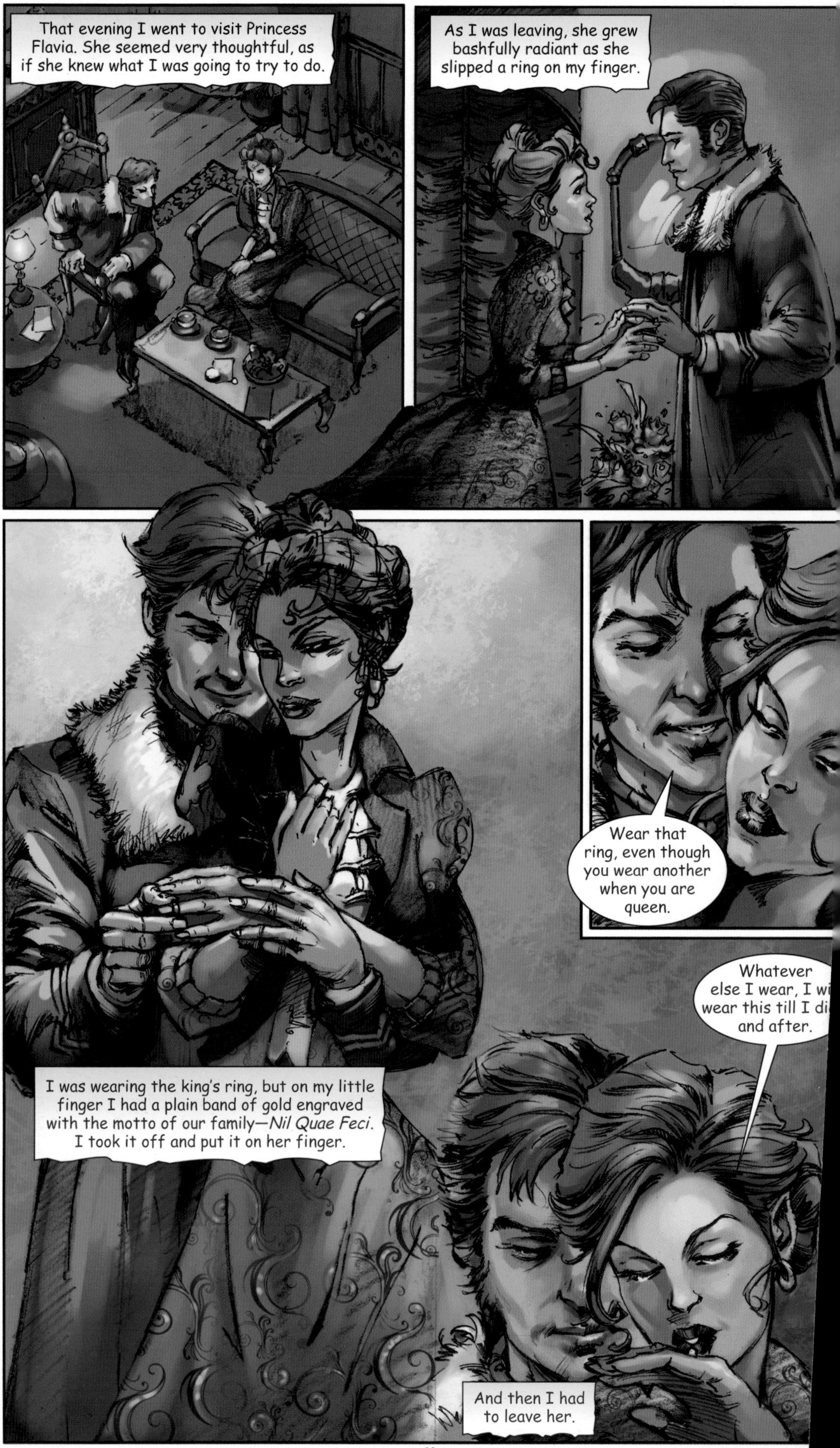
That evening I went to visit Princess Flavia. She seemed very thoughtful, as if she knew what I was going to try to do.
As I was leaving, she grew bashfully radiant as she slipped a ring on my finger.
Wear that ring, even though you wear another when you are queen.
Whatever else I wear, I wi wear this till I di and after.
I was wearing the king's ring, but on my little finger I had a plain band of gold engraved with the motto of our family—*Nil Quae Feci*. I took it off and put it on her finger.
And then I had to leave her.

At midnight, Sapt, Fritz and their men left, riding to the castle. If all went well, they would be waiting when Johann opened the castle door.

Taking another route, I also left Tarlenheim. When I reached the moat, I tied my horse up in a thick clump of trees. I unwound my rope from my waist, bound it securely around the trunk of a tree on the bank and let myself down into the water.

I crouched down in the shadow of the great pipe, waiting to put my plan into action. Light was coming from Duke Michael's window across the moat and I could see into the room.

Then Madame de Mauban came to the window... with Rupert of Hentzau behind her!

Hang Black Michael. Isn't the princess enough for him? What the devil do you see in him?

If I told him what you say--

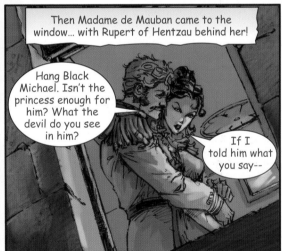

What are you doing here?

Apologizing for your absence, Could I leave the lady alone?

There is room for more than just the king in the moat. Please sir, leave us.

Rupert soon crossed the drawbridge. Not long after, it was drawn up. The light went out in Michael's room, but another light came on in the room next to his—Antoinette's.

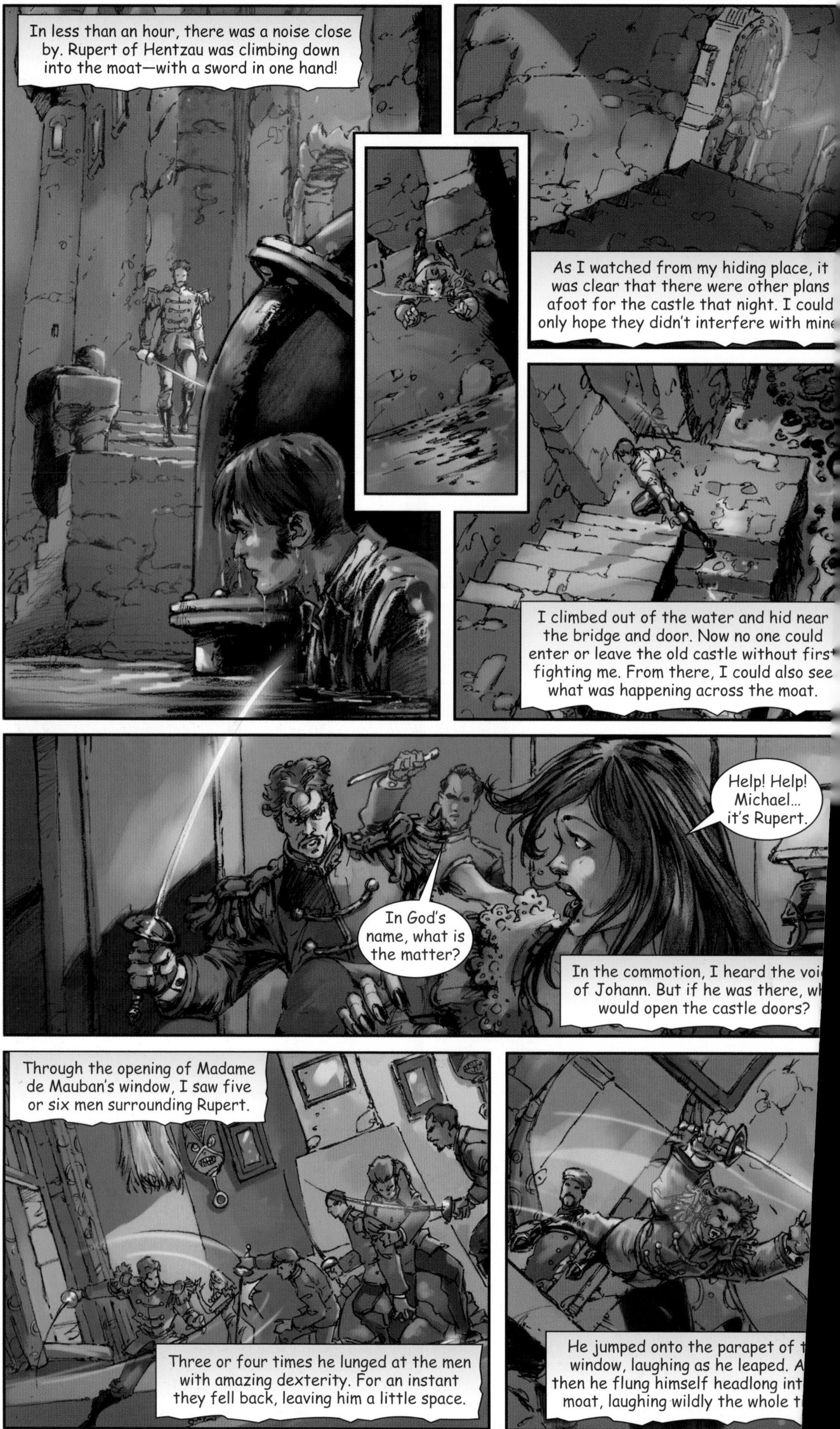
In less than an hour, there was a noise close by. Rupert of Hentzau was climbing down into the moat—with a sword in one hand!
As I watched from my hiding place, it was clear that there were other plans afoot for the castle that night. I could only hope they didn't interfere with mine
I climbed out of the water and hid near the bridge and door. Now no one could enter or leave the old castle without first fighting me. From there, I could also see what was happening across the moat.
Help! Help! Michael... it's Rupert.
In God's name, what is the matter?
In the commotion, I heard the voi of Johann. But if he was there, wh would open the castle doors?
Through the opening of Madame de Mauban's window, I saw five or six men surrounding Rupert.
Three or four times he lunged at the men with amazing dexterity. For an instant they fell back, leaving him a little space.
He jumped onto the parapet of t window, laughing as he leaped. A then he flung himself headlong int moat, laughing wildly the whole ti

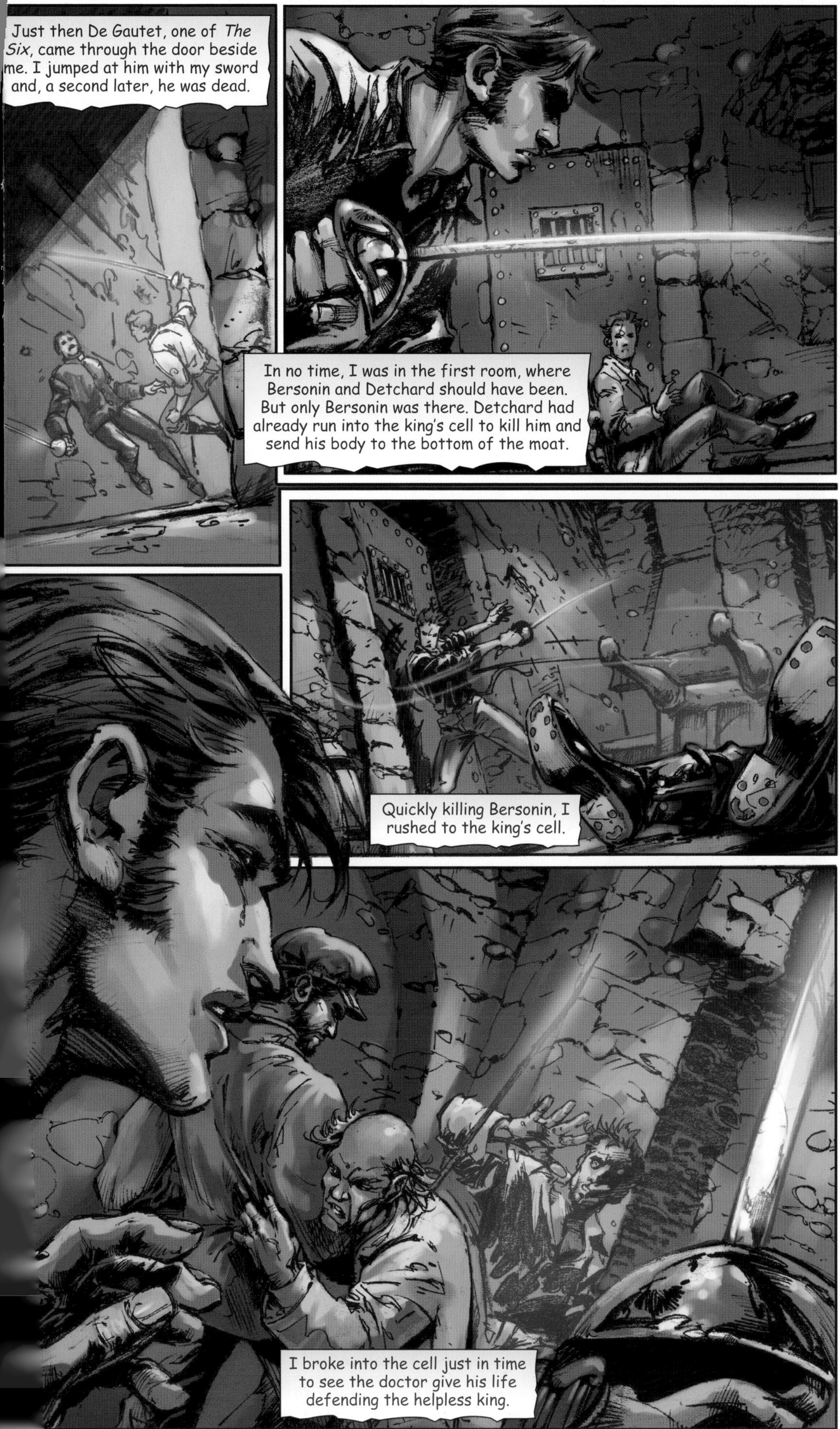
Just then De Gautet, one of *The Six*, came through the door beside me. I jumped at him with my sword and, a second later, he was dead.
In no time, I was in the first room, where Bersonin and Detchard should have been. But only Bersonin was there. Detchard had already run into the king's cell to kill him and send his body to the bottom of the moat.
Quickly killing Bersonin, I rushed to the king's cell.
I broke into the cell just in time to see the doctor give his life defending the helpless king.

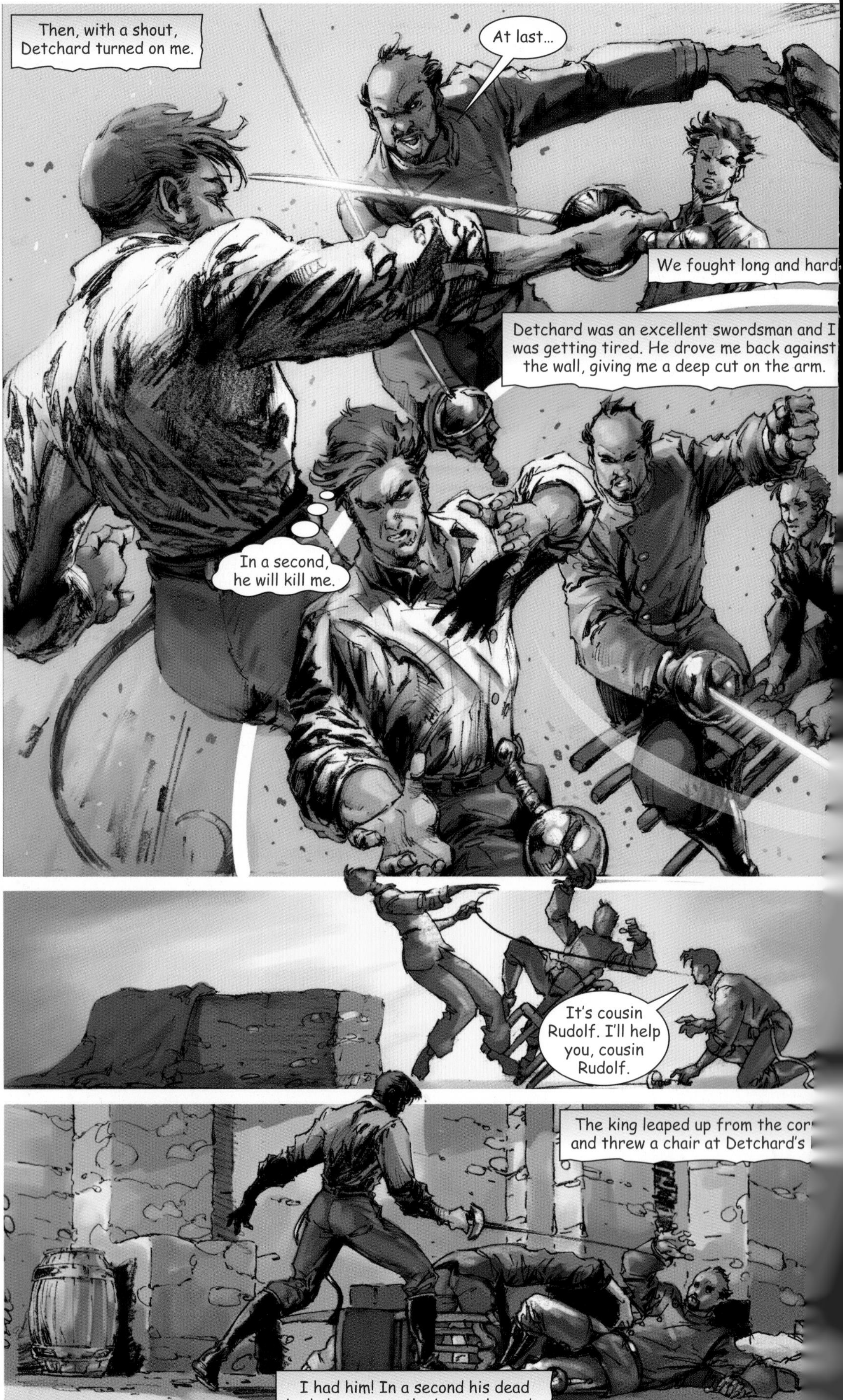

Then, with a shout, Detchard turned on me.
At last...
We fought long and hard
Detchard was an excellent swordsman and I was getting tired. He drove me back against the wall, giving me a deep cut on the arm.
In a second, he will kill me.
It's cousin Rudolf. I'll help you, cousin Rudolf.
The king leaped up from the cor and threw a chair at Detchard's
I had him! In a second his dead body lay across the brave doctor's.

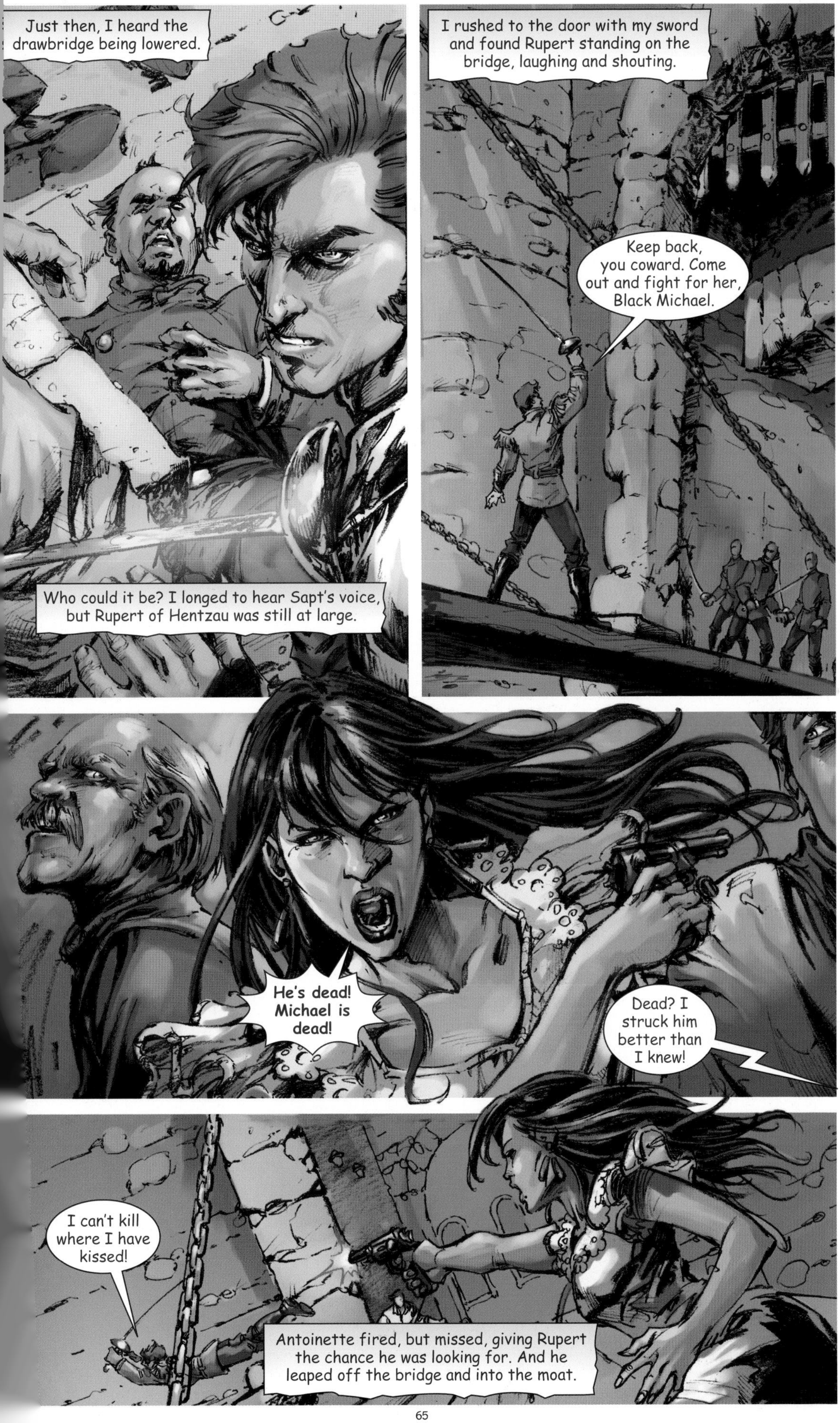

Just then, I heard the drawbridge being lowered.
Who could it be? I longed to hear Sapt's voice, but Rupert of Hentzau was still at large.
I rushed to the door with my sword and found Rupert standing on the bridge, laughing and shouting.
Keep back, you coward. Come out and fight for her, Black Michael.
He's dead! Michael is dead!
Dead? I struck him better than I knew!
I can't kill where I have kissed!
Antoinette fired, but missed, giving Rupert the chance he was looking for. And he leaped off the bridge and into the moat.

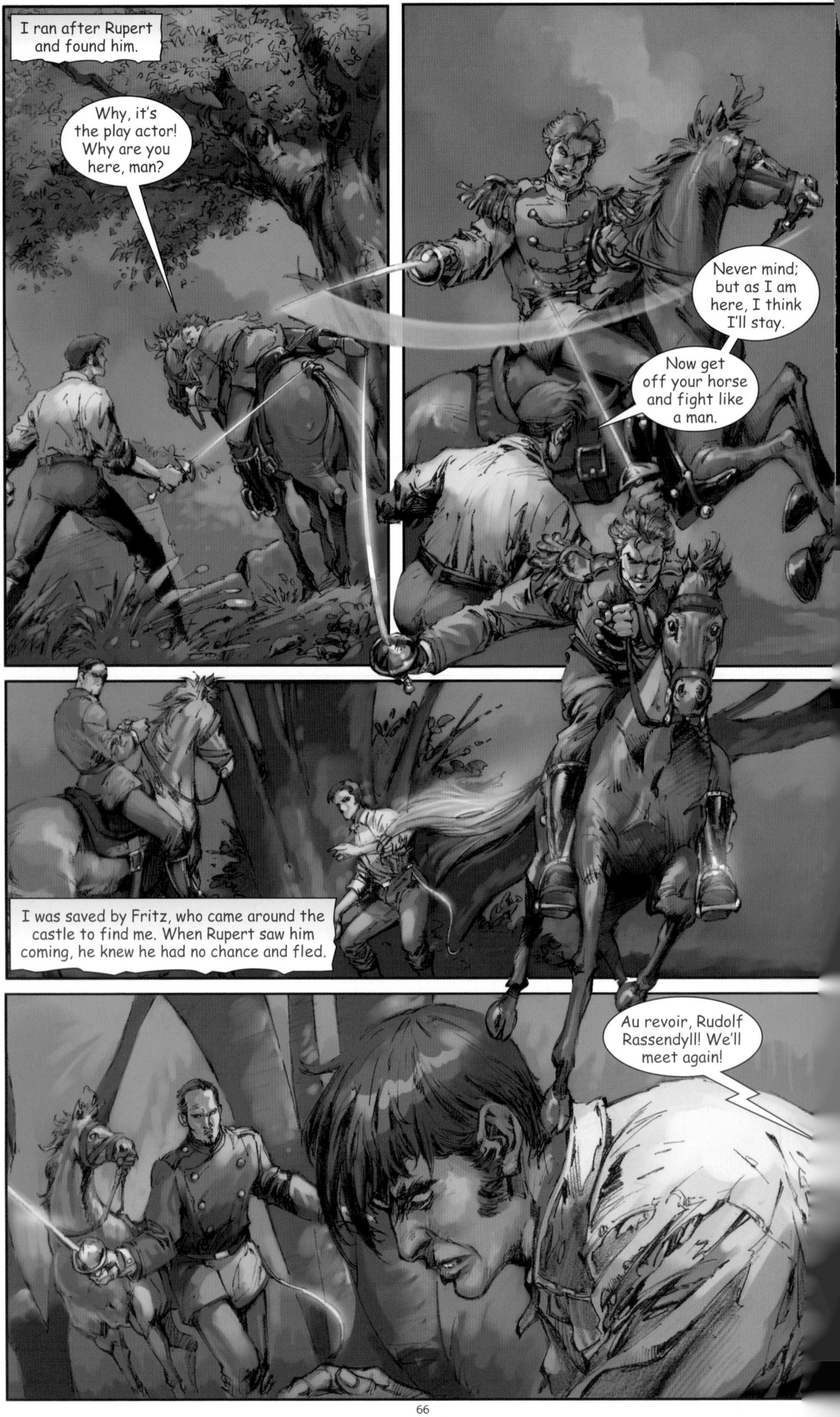

I ran after Rupert and found him.
Why, it's the play actor! Why are you here, man?
Never mind; but as I am here, I think I'll stay.
Now get off your horse and fight like a man.
I was saved by Fritz, who came around the castle to find me. When Rupert saw him coming, he knew he had no chance and fled.
Au revoir, Rudolf Rassendyll! We'll meet again!

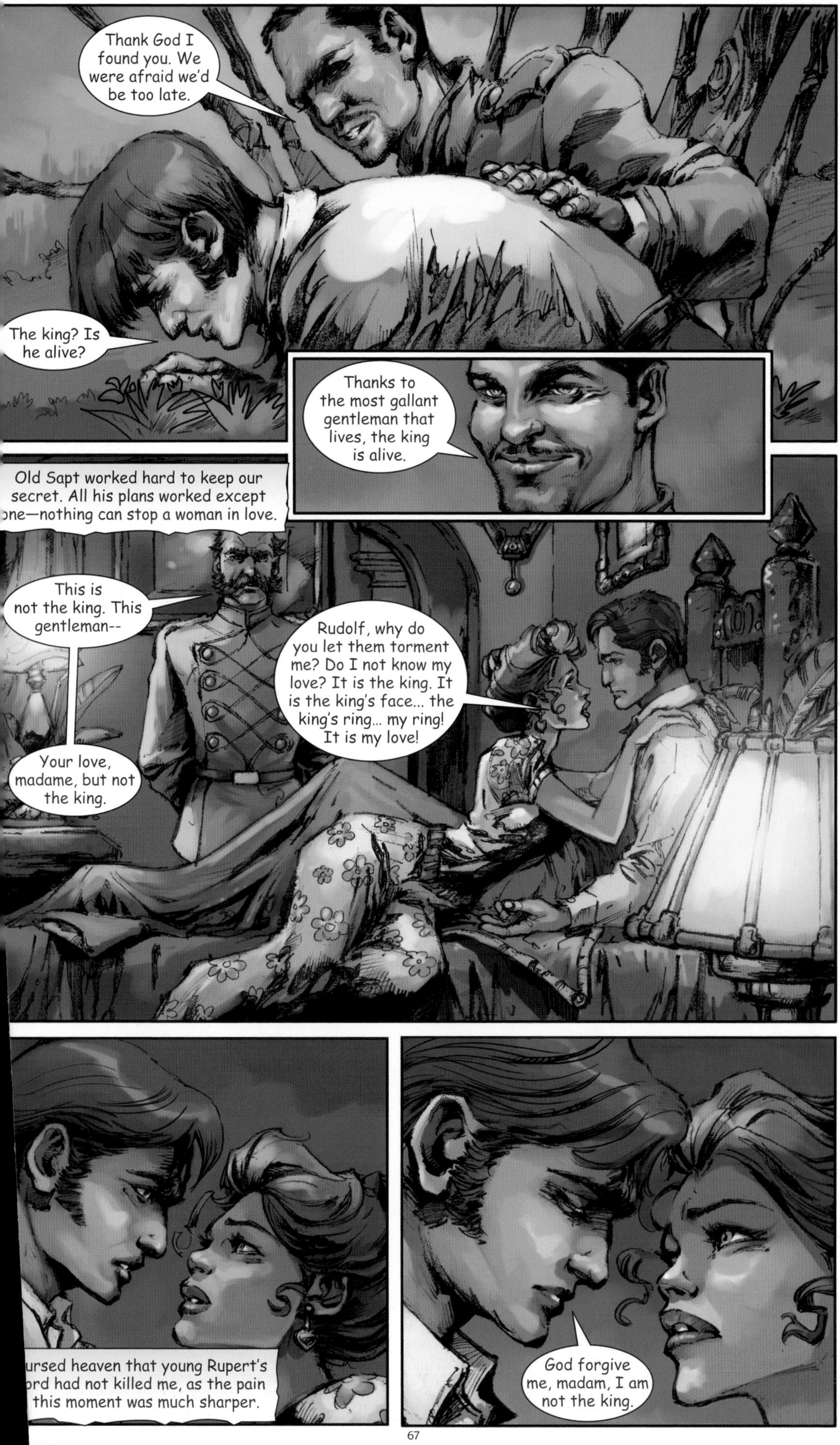
Thank God I found you. We were afraid we'd be too late.
The king? Is he alive?
Thanks to the most gallant gentleman that lives, the king is alive.
Old Sapt worked hard to keep our secret. All his plans worked except one—nothing can stop a woman in love.
This is not the king. This gentleman--
Your love, madame, but not the king.
Rudolf, why do you let them torment me? Do I not know my love? It is the king. It is the king's face... the king's ring... my ring! It is my love!
ursed heaven that young Rupert's ord had not killed me, as the pain this moment was much sharper.
God forgive me, madam, I am not the king.

I saw the king once more. He thanked me and I returned the royal Elphberg ring. If he had noticed my ring on the princess's hand, he said nothing.

I have tried not to dishonor the ring, sir.

I wanted to take you to Strelsau and keep you with me, and tell everyone of what you have done. If that were possible, you would have been my best and nearest friend, cousin Rudolf. But they tell me I must not, and that the secret must be kept.

I saw Flavia one final time.

Rudolf... Rudolf... what are we to do? I know my honor lies in being true to my country. I don't know why God has let me love you, but I know that I must stay.

I am going away tonight. You are my queen and my beauty, and always will be.

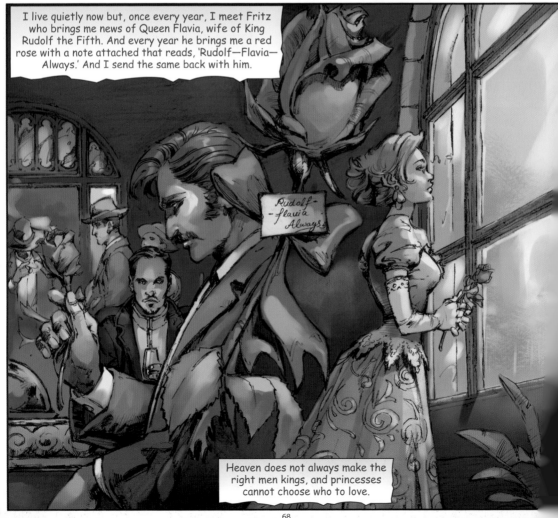

I live quietly now but, once every year, I meet Fritz who brings me news of Queen Flavia, wife of King Rudolf the Fifth. And every year he brings me a red rose with a note attached that reads, 'Rudolf—Flavia—Always.' And I send the same back with him.

Rudolf—
—Flavia—
Always

Heaven does not always make the right men kings, and princesses cannot choose who to love.

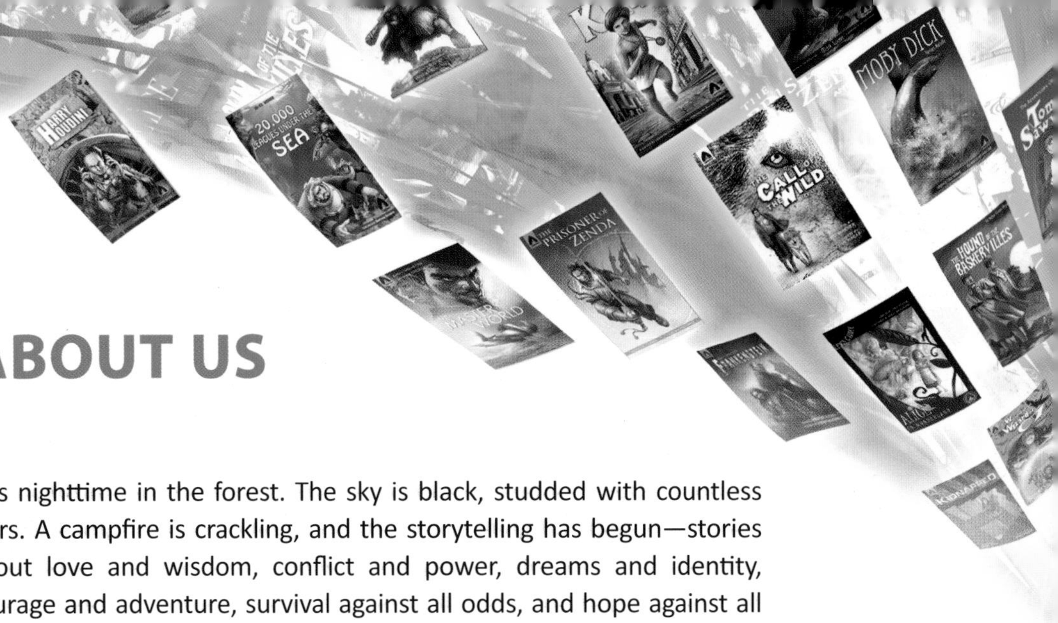
HARRY HOUDINI
20,000 LEAGUES UNDER THE SEA
MOBY DICK
THE CALL OF THE WILD
THE PRISONER OF ZENDA
THE HOUND OF THE BASKERVILLES
KIDNAPPED

ABOUT US

It is nighttime in the forest. The sky is black, studded with countless stars. A campfire is crackling, and the storytelling has begun—stories about love and wisdom, conflict and power, dreams and identity, courage and adventure, survival against all odds, and hope against all hope. In the warm, cheerful radiance of the campfire, the storyteller's audience is captivated, as in a trance. Even the trees and the earth and the animals of the forest seem to have fallen silent, bewitched.

Inspired by this enduring relationship between a campfire and gripping storytelling, we bring you four series of *Campfire Graphic Novels*:

Our *Classic* tales adapt timeless literature from some of the greatest writers ever.

Our *Mythology* series features epics, myths and legends from around the world, tales that transport readers to lands of mystery and magic.

Our *Biography* titles bring to life remarkable and inspiring figures from history.

Our *Original* line showcases brand new characters and stories from some of today's most talented graphic novelists and illustrators.

We hope you will gather around our campfire and discover the fascinating stories and characters inside our books.

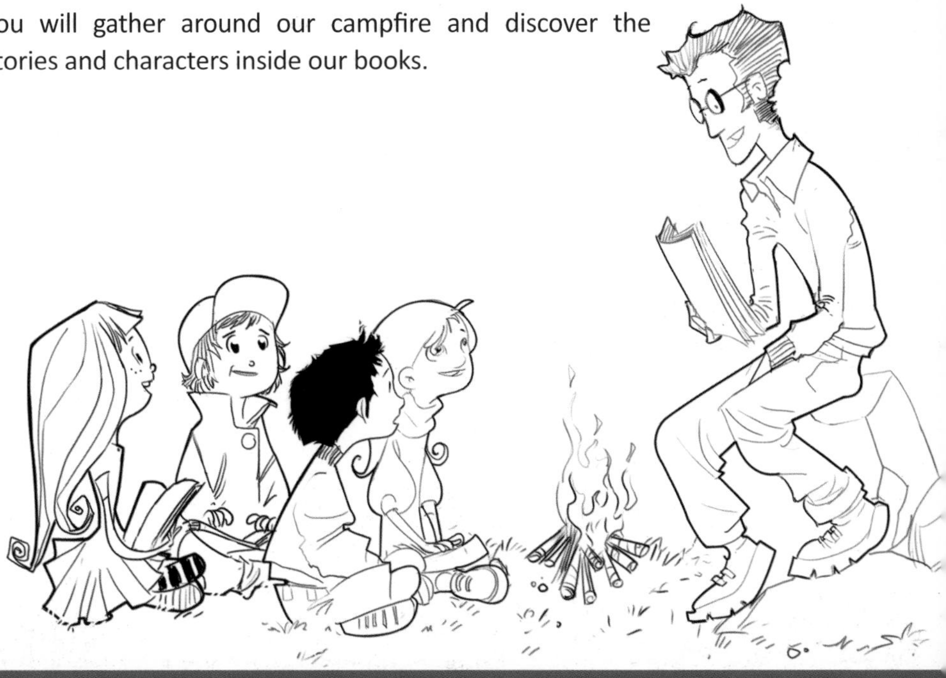

CAMPFIRE™

Royal Residence

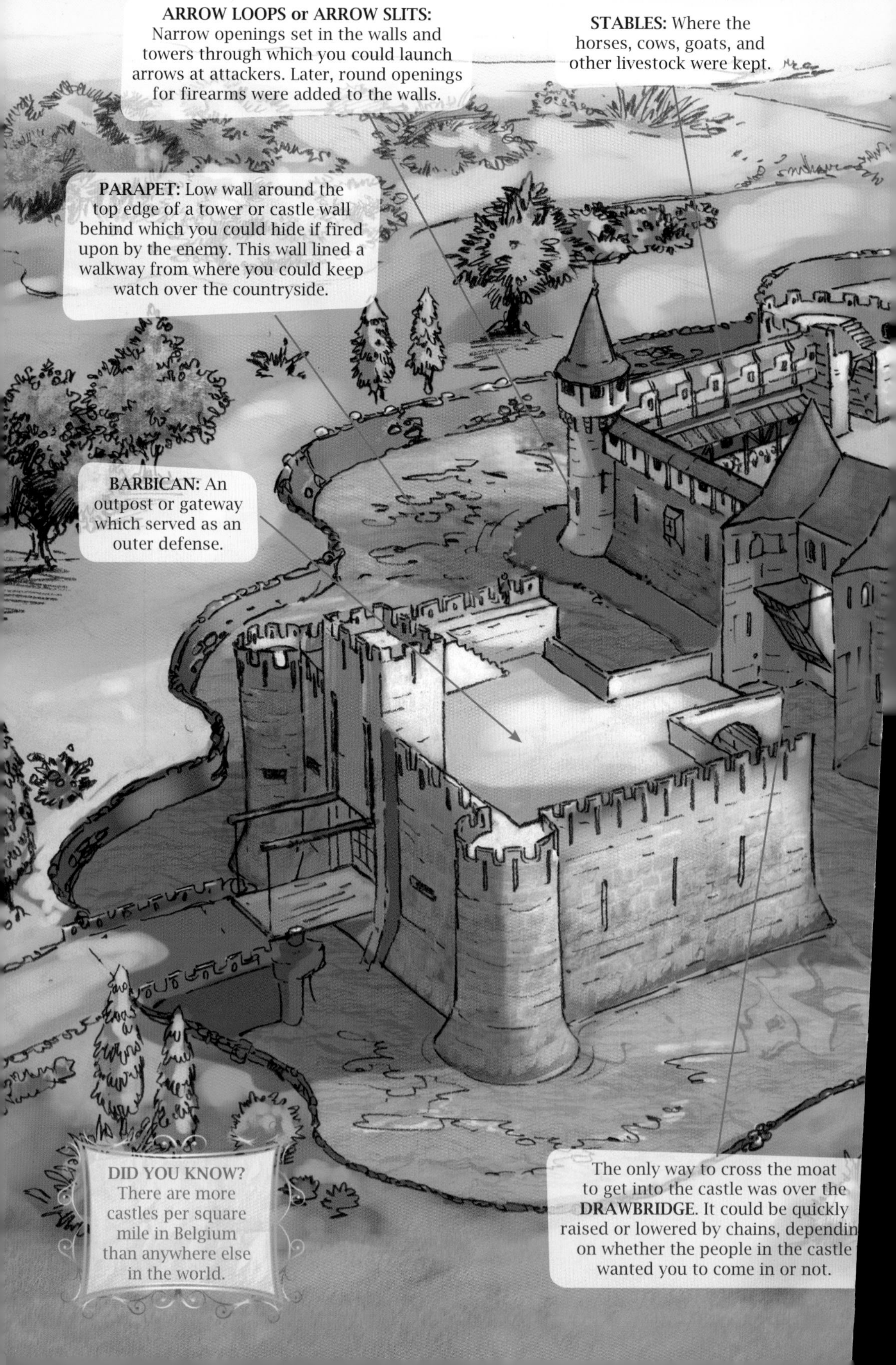

ARROW LOOPS or ARROW SLITS: Narrow openings set in the walls and towers through which you could launch arrows at attackers. Later, round openings for firearms were added to the walls.
STABLES: Where the horses, cows, goats, and other livestock were kept.
PARAPET: Low wall around the top edge of a tower or castle wall behind which you could hide if fired upon by the enemy. This wall lined a walkway from where you could keep watch over the countryside.
BARBICAN: An outpost or gateway which served as an outer defense.
DID YOU KNOW? There are more castles per square mile in Belgium than anywhere else in the world.
The only way to cross the moat to get into the castle was over the **DRAWBRIDGE**. It could be quickly raised or lowered by chains, dependin on whether the people in the castle wanted you to come in or not.

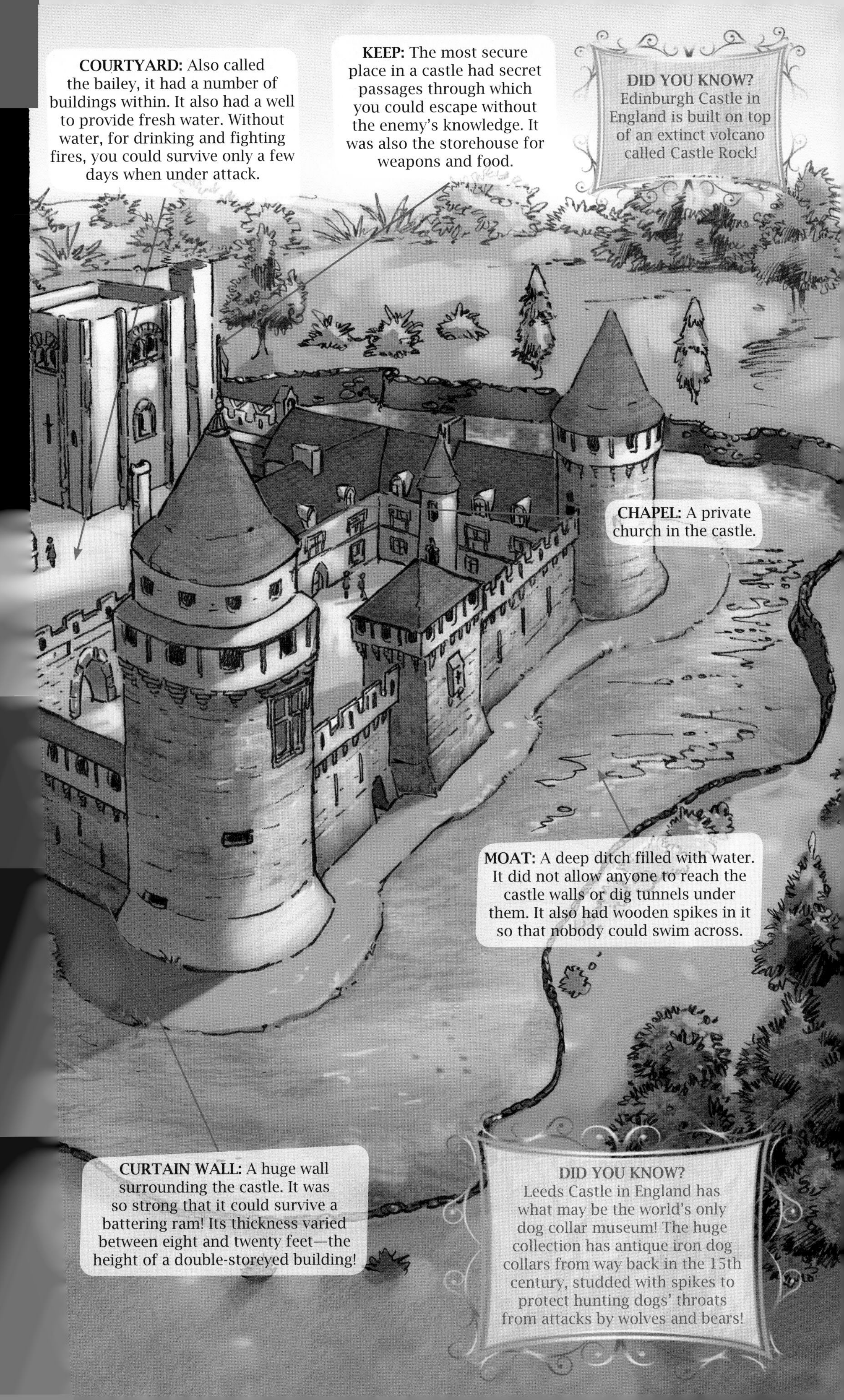
COURTYARD: Also called the bailey, it had a number of buildings within. It also had a well to provide fresh water. Without water, for drinking and fighting fires, you could survive only a few days when under attack.
KEEP: The most secure place in a castle had secret passages through which you could escape without the enemy's knowledge. It was also the storehouse for weapons and food.
DID YOU KNOW? Edinburgh Castle in England is built on top of an extinct volcano called Castle Rock!
CHAPEL: A private church in the castle.
MOAT: A deep ditch filled with water. It did not allow anyone to reach the castle walls or dig tunnels under them. It also had wooden spikes in it so that nobody could swim across.
CURTAIN WALL: A huge wall surrounding the castle. It was so strong that it could survive a battering ram! Its thickness varied between eight and twenty feet—the height of a double-storeyed building!
DID YOU KNOW? Leeds Castle in England has what may be the world's only dog collar museum! The huge collection has antique iron dog collars from way back in the 15th century, studded with spikes to protect hunting dogs' throats from attacks by wolves and bears!

ALSO AVAILABLE FROM
CAMPFIRE GRAPHIC NOVELS

CAMPFIRE™

ROBINSON CRUSOE

A CHRISTMAS CAROL

THE ADVENTURES OF Tom Sawyer

THE MASTER OF THE WORLD

THE LOST CONTINENT

THE CALL OF THE WILD

THE TIME MACHINE
H.G. WELLS

THE ADVENTURES OF HUCKLEBERRY FINN

FRANKENSTEIN

THE PRISONER OF ZENDA

THE INVISIBLE MAN

LEGEND

HARRY HOUDINI

MOBY DICK

TREASURE ISLAND

ALICE IN WONDERLAND

Putting the fun back into reading!

Explore the latest from Campfire at
www.campfire.co.in